3615 CODE SANTA CLAUS

the official novelisation by
CHRISTIAN FRANCIS

based on *3615 Code Père Noël* by
RENE MANZOR

ECHO ON PUBLISHING

Every child believes in magic, and he stops doing so when he grows up (with the exception of those who have been too disappointed in reality to be able to trust its rewards).

Bruno Bettelheim
The Uses of Enchantment: The Meaning and Importance of Fairy Tales

PROLOGUE

On a snowy street in the third arrondissement of Paris stood an elegant Haussmann-style apartment, a building that had seen much better days. Its wrought-iron balconies were draped with plants, some thriving, others brittle and brown. The once-pristine limestone façade had aged over the decades and was now cracked and grayed. Inside, the smell of damp wood gripped the corridors, as the marble stairs stood steep and neglected. Not many of the residents used them anymore, favouring the apartment's elevator. Yet even that was a relic from another era. Its metal doors were dented, and its grimy frosted glass distorted any shapes wherever they were inside. As it moved, it rattled loudly, sounding on the verge of breaking with each floor it passed.

At the end of each corridor on every floor, morning light shone weakly through the ornamental stained-glass windows, casting a variety of coloured streaks across the faded wallpaper and threadbare carpet. At this hour, the building was quiet. It was still too early for most of the elderly residents to be awake and out of their homes. But for the few younger ones who lived there, it was just the beginning of their day.

Up on the second floor, a keyring dangled in the eight-year-old girl's hands as she fumbled to lock her family's front door. On her way to school, she had a satchel slung over her shoulder that was almost too big, and certainly too heavy, packed with all her classes' textbooks.

Her long, neatly parted braids swung gently as she walked, and the heels on her leather shoes clacked on the tiled floor.

Down on the ground level, the resident's entrance clicked as a man opened it then stepped out into the snow. But just before the latch could shut again, a man had slipped by and gotten inside. A man who did not live here. A man looking for some warmth from the winter outside.

Tall and broad-shouldered, this man wore an old beige woollen coat, and kept his head low beneath a dark cap. His cheeks were flushed from cold, as around his neck, a bright yellow scarf was wrapped loosely. A spot of brightness on an otherwise shadowy figure.

He stood by the radiator, rubbing his gloved hands together, shivering and feeling all the heat he could.

He hoped not to be noticed here. That he could come in, get warm and leave without a second glance. After spending another night sleeping in the snow, he only wanted to feel his fingers again. He did not want any trouble.

As the feeling started to come back to his fingers, he heard a noise.

From above, the sound of small footsteps could be heard. He looked up and caught a fleeting glimpse of the little girl skipping past the stairwell's opening and over to the elevator.

He smiled as he noticed her.

The elevator sat on the ground floor, its doors slightly ajar from the last resident's use. With a silent excitement, the man walked over and got inside. Pressing himself into the corner, with a childlike grin on his face, as if preparing for a surprise.

Above, the little girl pressed the call button and waited. As with every morning, she briefly considered taking the stairs before opting for the elevator instead. She hummed, distracted by thoughts of school and the cursive writing test her teacher had threatened them with. Her breath was visible in a chill that had crept in from the lobby below, and she pulled her coat in tighter.

The call button soon stopped its blinking, and with a soft ding, the elevator doors slid open.

There stood the man. He didn't move. He didn't speak. He simply smiled at her. A wide and gentle smile.

She didn't know his name, but the man looked kind. He also looked a bit sad. She thought, maybe if she smiled at him, he wouldn't feel so lonely.

The elevator clacked, shuddered, and began its descent.

The man stayed in his corner, ever silent.

But as she peered up at him, he raised his fist slowly, like he'd seen other children do.

Rock.

Then changed to paper.

Then to scissors.

His smile widened, proud of himself. He remembered this game. His eyebrows raised playfully, eyes alight with happy anticipation.

The girl looked back, confused. She didn't respond. She just sneered as she turned away, dropping her eyes to the floor.

Why didn't she want to play? He thought. He

was nice. He had smiled. He did it right this time. Not like before.

The silence between them became thicker. She fidgeted with the strap of her satchel, wanting to get out of the elevator and get to school.

The man felt her rejection as the lightness in his expression drained, replaced by upset, then brought with it something much darker. A deep anger.

His hand lunged as he grabbed her arm, desperate to get her attention, but she pulled away too fast.

Then something in him snapped. Just like before.

From the elevator, there was only a single scream, followed by a gasp and the frantic tapping of heels against a metal floor.

With a loud chime, the doors slid open on the ground floor, and the man stumbled out, his scarf flaring up behind him.

His chest heaved. His eyes were wild. His face was pale.

His hands trembled as they were held out, clutching nothing but air.

He only wanted to play...

He didn't look back.

He fled back through the residents' entrance again and disappeared into the waking city beyond.

Above, a few apartment doors creaked open.

"Did you hear that?" a woman called out down the corridor, her robe pulled tightly against the chill.

"Yes," someone else replied. "What was it? Was it a scream?"

Another resident peered out from a floor below. "I heard it too."

Down the stairwell, a man descended in his slippers, still brushing shaving foam away from his chin. Assuming the sound had come from the street, he opened the door and peered outside. But there was nothing there except the dull crunch of snow and the distant hum of morning traffic. He sighed and closed the door.

Turning to return upstairs, he paused. The elevator doors stood half open, trying to close over and over.

Something was blocking them.

As he approached, he saw the satchel. Its contents had spilled across the threshold.

He then saw her.

One hand moved to his mouth in shock. "Oh my god..." was all he could mutter.

More voices followed. More doors opened. The building began to stir.

There, in the corner of the elevator, slumped awkwardly, was the small girl's body. Silent and still.

Outside, Paris moved on. Buses hissed. Cars crept on as traffic built up. People walked beneath bundled scarves and fogged up glasses. The city continued through the cold, unaware of what had just ended.

CHAPTER ONE

The manor house looked solemn in the cold morning light. Its stone walls held the wear of too many seasons, and was a building that had seen much better days. It was not neglected at all, but it certainly was frayed around the edges.

In the gym room on the first floor, one of the weight benches clanged and thudded beneath the efforts of a boy. He was far too young to know what real combat was or felt like, but he was training as if he was preparing for one.

Thomas de Frémont was ten years old. With army-green trousers hanging low on his hips, his bare chest dripped with what looked like sweat, but had instead come from a tap. An old radio headset was cupped over his ears, as rock music blared out. He did not smile. His expression was just stern and focused.

The weight machines clanked as he pulled on the handlebars, then when his reps were done, he worked his way to the next, not pausing to rest between the sets. Five rapid arm curls, five stomach crunches, then the whine of the rowing machine's flywheel as he worked out for five minutes to the music's beat. Then, as he dropped to the floor for five push-ups, he was not there alone.

A long tongue came in from one side, and before Thomas could stop it, licked his face with a line of wet slobber.

"Hey, stop it!" he complained, breathless but serious, as J.R., his shaggy dog stared lovingly back. "You can see I'm training!"

J.R., ignored the command and licked Thomas again, his tail busily thumping on the hardwood floor happily.

Shaking his head, realizing he could not carry on, Thomas sat up.

"Well, you asked for it," he shrugged. "It's *that* time."

Hurriedly, he got up and picked up a walkie-talkie from a windowsill. Clipping it to J.R.'s collar, he then ushered the dog out of the room.

"You better be ready!" Thomas said as he walked

the other way, down the stairs into the bottom of the house.

Then came his ritual. The thing he had done many times and had down to an almost art form.

First came the black T-shirt. It went over his head and was tucked tight into his camouflage trousers' waistband. Then, a red scarf was wrapped and tied with precision around his forehead. Picking up a harness, he strapped it over each arm, and sheathed into the slot on the back, was a long plastic toy sword. A single black glove was slipped onto his left hand, the right left bare. Around his chest, two criss-crossed belts of toy arrows with suction-cup tips on them. Around his waist, he buckled a wide belt, heavy with absurd but carefully selected gear: plastic handcuffs, small binoculars, a foam grenade, and his own walkie-talkie. Then came the plastic survival knife, jammed into the belt's scabbard.

As the final touch, he dipped two fingers into a tin of black shoe polish and smeared lines across his arms and face, like he was going to be battling in the jungle.

Even with this, his game was not quite ready yet. He was dressed, but the scene still needed to be set.

He removed his headset and slid a tape cassette into an old tape player nearby. One with lots of cables trailing from the back and disappearing into the wall. The cassette had a title written in marker pen on its front: *Noises of War*.

Thomas hit the play button.

Speakers hidden throughout the manor house then crackled to life, unleashing a barrage of sounds: machine gun fire, screaming jet engines, distant explosions. The soundtrack to this boy's playtime battles.

Picking up his plastic Kalashnikov, Thomas soon emerged and ascended into the first-floor hallway and pushed himself against the wall, hiding from an imagined enemy. There was no one in sight, but he was still careful. He sneaked across the wood-panelled hall and ducked behind a large houseplant, careful not to make a single sound.

He grabbed his walkie-talkie, pulled its antenna up, and listened to its speaker. There was only static heard. Then a faint whine and a jingle of tags.

It was J.R.

The walkie-talkie was hearing sounds over the open channel from the one clipped on the dog's collar.

With a smile, Thomas lowered the antenna and hung the device back on his belt. Suddenly, he was on the move again, quick and light on his feet.

Stopping at the ajar door to his own bedroom.

He kicked it open, unleashing a burst of clacking toy gunfire from the Kalashnikov.

RAT TAT TAT TAT TAT.

The war noises coming from the speakers on the walls added to the racket.

But his bedroom was empty. There was no enemy here.

He immediately dropped to the floor and rolled under the bed.

He crawled on his elbows until he reached the other side, and stood up by the window on the other side. With practiced care, he opened it and climbed outside onto the balcony.

It was bitingly cold as he walked along the ledge, pushing his back against the building's outer wall. He ignored the chill and continued with determination. He edged along the narrow stone cornice, a sheer six meters dropped to the garden below. He had to steady himself before he slipped, but as he did, his Kalashnikov slipped from his grip, clattering as it bounced off the ledge and tumbled down, far down to the grass below.

Thomas teetered for a second. His arms flailed as it looked like he might follow the gun's descent... *Not today*, he told himself.

In his mind, he was on the edge of a large drop. This was a perilous mission after all.

The truth, though, was that he was not in any danger at all. He was standing on a wide stone balcony, with a large balustrade in front of him. But for the sake of Thomas' game, it may as well have been a mountain cliff.

When he reached the next window, he climbed back over the frame and slipped silently into the manor house once more.

His game was only just starting.

The moment Thomas re-entered the house, he was confronted with his enemy. An enemy now licking their own behind, sat by the doorway.

Thomas silently unclipped his toy sawn-off shotgun, levelled it and took aim.

He squeezed the trigger, firing at his dog.

A suction-cupped arrow flew from the gun, through the air and struck J.R. on the chest. Not hard, but enough to make the dog stop cleaning itself, and get up and slowly walk out of the room.

Thomas holstered his weapon with satisfaction, then launched himself upward and grabbed hold of the low-hanging chandelier. He swung himself forward, letting go just above his grandfather's bed, bounced off the mattress with a practiced step, and landed by the door.

His grandfather, Papy, aged in his seventies, didn't stir. He had been woken up many times before, to Thomas' battles, but now he was used to the morning noise and remained snoring beneath his blanket.

Down the corridor, J.R. had made a break for the grand staircase, and Thomas was giving chase. He closed the gap, pausing only long enough to grab two Velcro-covered plastic throwing stars from his belt. With a swift overhand, he flung both stars at the dog, and both found their mark. They attached to J.R.'s fur, looking like matador banderillas hanging from a bull. The dog glanced back with his tongue out, greatly enjoying their morning game.

Thomas reached for his samurai sword, drew it, then spun it around his body in two tight flourishes.

Still playing in the background, the war soundtrack persisted through the wall-mounted speakers.

J.R. bounded down the staircase, his paws tapping on the wood.

Thomas, though, took the quicker route, sliding down the polished banister as if he were on a zipline.

When he landed at the bottom, the dog had already bolted across the lobby.

Thomas slowed, his sword at the ready. He moved in slow circles around a suit of armor that stood at one end of the room, peering behind it with an exaggerated suspicion. Around the large brightly lit Christmas tree. But the enemy combatant had gotten free.

He lowered the plastic blade and sheathed it back onto his back. Then he pulled up the antenna on his walkie-talkie, and listened to the speaker intently. Waiting to hear the dog's noises.

A burst of sound then came through. Familiar tags jingling, but also a churning noise of water and machinery.

"I *know* where you are!" Thomas said gleefully.

Down in the laundry room on the first level of the sub-basement, the sound from the washing machines were louder than the sounds of war playing upstairs. In this room, the dog wandered down and meandered between the suspended sheets hanging on the clotheslines, sniffing about as he walked.

Thomas' voice crackled through the radio on his collar. *You're in the laundry room. And I have a little surprise for you.'*

Thomas was back upstairs. He moved quickly, piling cushions to form a small barricade. When it was done, he rolled back a long Persian rug that covered the parquet flooring. Beneath it lay a new addition to his wargames. One Thomas had built himself over the past month. A trap door, about six feet long, its edges freshly cut, its hinges oiled and ready. A trap door that neither his mother nor grandfather had given permission to be made, but one they did not speak up about when they found out about.

As Thomas prepared his new trap, he kept the walkie-talkie on, attached to his belt, listening for more signs of movement.

Soon, J.R.'s signal left the churning noise of the washing machines and was replaced by the sound of his paws padding along wood. Then upstairs. Then along wood again.

Thomas smiled. J.R. was heading straight for him, as he always did. The dog always followed the same route as he walked around the house. It was only a matter of time before he would appear around the corner ahead.

Thomas dropped behind his barricade and peered down the hallway through a small pair of toy binoculars.

In his other hand, he held a remote control with a large red button in the middle of it.

A minute later, totally expected, the dog emerged, happily wagging his tail.

Thomas' thumb hovered over the red button.

Seeing his owner, J.R. bounded forward, without a care in the world, just enjoying playtime, happy to see Thomas.

Much like everyone else, J.R. had no idea about the trap door recently cut into the hallway floorboards.

With a grin, Thomas pressed the red button as J.R. hit a certain spot, and immediately the boards underneath its legs gave way, and he vanished below with a startled yelp.

Thomas triumphantly raised a plastic grenade in his hand, pulled the pin and lobbed it toward the hole where his enemy lay.

It flew in a perfect arc. But before it could land, a hand reached and plucked it from the air, mid-flight.

Julie, Thomas' mother, stood staring at him, dressed in a pinstripe suit. A disappointed frown was on her face, as she looked at the trap door.

"Breakfast is ready," she said with a shake of her head. "Now, go wake up your grandfather."

She stepped forward, and peered down through the trap door. She saw the dog lying in a net, looking a bit startled, but happily lying down. Not scared or hurt in the slightest.

She sighed, yet could not bring herself to say anything to Thomas about this. He was happiest playing his games, and she would do anything to keep him happy. To keep him distracted.

"Please, get the dog out of there," she said as she walked away to the dining room.

Thomas didn't argue. He smiled, and walked over to get J.R.

When the dog was carried out of the hole, the war had paused for now. As now was the start of the next mission... Operation Papy.

He ran back down the stairs into the cellar.

Careful to check that no one was following him, Thomas crept into one of the basement's side rooms and approached an old refrigerator that sat in the shadows at the far end.

Opening its door, he was not met with a rack of food or drink as you would expect, just a dark hole. One that he quickly disappeared into.

Descending a staircase made of warped old wood, Thomas flicked on the light switch, and the expansive room below him lit up. This was his base. His *secret* base. His sanctuary. One filled with toys and gadgets.

This was a room that always brought memories of his father. This hidden room had been his, and before that, his father's, and his grandfather's before him. Passed down through generations of de Frémont men, and now it belonged to Thomas.

So well-hidden was the room, that Thomas doubted anyone aside from him knew of its existence, and he intended to keep it that way. Some things were not meant to be shared.

Yet it was also a place of sadness. The room carried ghosts of many childhoods. Toys and games that belonged to each man as they grew up. From teddy bears to toy guns. And as Thomas' mother ran a department store, the many toys she brought home eventually made their way down here as well. Pushed on shelves covering all the older ones, all to try and block out the memory of—

No. He couldn't afford to dwell on what happened to his father now. He had Operation Papy.

Running past a row of shelves, he moved over to his command center, a large bank of electronic equipment, all joined together by a mess of tangled wires and cables. Battered speakers, old reel-to-reel players, microphones. All scavenged tech that had been cobbled together to make many other devices. Every part of which was built by Thomas. He may have been very young, but he knew how to make things. From trap doors to speaker loops, to computer-run devices.... anything that he imagined, he somehow managed to bring to life.

As he switched off the tape recorder, the *Noises of War* soundtrack cut out, and the speakers throughout the manor house fell silent.

Up in the dining room, Julie breathed a sigh of relief that those noises had stopped.

Thomas then reached for another panel, twisting knobs and connecting wires with precision. He picked up the microphone and pressed its talk button.

He took a breath before he shouted, "Rise and shine, soldier!"

Upstairs, in his grandfather's room, Thomas' voice came shrieking through a speaker.

Papy was forcibly woken by the loud noise.

A couple of minutes later, Thomas kicked open his grandfather's bedroom door and stormed in, plastic shotgun raised. He shouted his command again.

"Stand or I'll shoot you!"

Papy looked at him, then let out a tired laugh.

With a smile, Thomas lowered his weapon and

walked over to help his grandfather out of bed, on the way picking up the dressing robe from the chair.

As the old man chuckled, Thomas slipped one arm of the robe over his hand and quickly followed it with a plastic handcuff. Locking it around his wrist.

"There you go," Thomas said, beaming. "You're now my prisoner of war."

"What? I'm too old for that!" Papy playfully protested.

Thomas shook his head and leaned in, kissing his grandfather on the forehead. "You're never too old to be captured!"

The old man relented, "Well then, I guess I'm your prisoner."

"Come on," Thomas said with a wink. "Let's get some breakfast!"

Paris, its rooftops crowned in snow like icing on a cake, looked impossibly still. Through every narrow alley and over each slanted rooftop, the city was perfect and beautiful. The Eiffel Tower stood in the distance, not just as a monument but as a dreamlike silhouette on the horizon.

Around, large snowflakes dropped dreamily down, swirling around the streets until they settled in a thick blanket.

This was a city captured in time. A city that rarely changed...

Until the garbage truck's tire came crashing down upon it. The illusion shattered. The picturesque city, miniature and delicate, collapsed beneath the vehicle's thick tread of rubber. The festive snow globe that held it all together exploded, scattering glitter and snow-dust in fragments across the icy street.

With schools soon starting for the day, the snow-covered side streets would be the domain of children playing, at least for the next twenty minutes.

A pair of small woollen mittens, red and damp at their fingertips, scooped a handful of snow from a bonnet of a parked car. The child pressed the snow together with a huge smile upon his face, before winding his arm back, ready to throw. But he had no time, as another snowball flew by him, missing his cheek by mere inches. It went careening past, and with a dull thud, exploded against the bottom edge of a large billboard stood behind him, sending a light dusting of flakes fluttering to the ground.

This billboard loomed above the street, its red colours were vibrant against the white of the winter morning. On it, a smiling illustration of Santa Claus beamed down, one hand raised in greeting, as below, bold letters read: *TYPE 36.15 CODE SANTA*

CLAUS. Speak to Santa today from the comfort of your own home.

The boy glanced at the impact mark for only a second before smiling and turning to hurl his own snowball back at his would-be attacker. Within a matter of moments, the two children who were throwing snowballs turned into a dozen, and the road became a laugher-filled battleground. There were no sides and no prizes.

Children crouched behind the shelter of parked cars, trees and lampposts, as shouts rang out between volleys of snow.

As these children played, a man walked by, glancing at them, at their happiness. Wishing he could be like that.

This man wearing a yellow scarf paused, watching intently with a hopeful expression. His face was half-hidden by the shadow of his hat, but when he smiled, it was boyish and innocent.

Then, as if on instinct, he reached down, scooped up a handful of snow, and packed it tight between his gloved fingers. He did not notice the shards of glass that he picked up along with the snow, remnants of the crushed snow globe.

Without hesitation, he threw himself into the game, his arm swinging forward as he released his snowball, then quickly bent to scoop up another.

The glass-packed ball barreled through the air, missing one child and slamming into a car nearby, the glass inside remained unnoticed as it clinked to the ground.

But the moment it had landed, the children's laughter stopped. Their excitement immediately evaporated, replaced by a quiet discomfort that a stranger had come into their game.

They hesitated as they exchanged knowing glances. One by one, they picked up their school bags, mumbled hurried apologies to each other, and left in small groups for their schools. None of them even looked back at the grown man who only wanted to play. They knew better than to talk to strangers, so they did what they had been taught to do: walk away.

The man in the yellow scarf stood alone and dejected for the second time that morning. He looked at the snowball in his hand and dropped it sadly to his feet.

As a feeling of anger built inside him, his gaze moved to the billboard of Santa Claus.

Smiling. Fat. Jolly. Loved by all.

Children would have played with him, the man thought.

TYPE 36.15 CODE SANTA CLAUS, it stated. And below, at the very bottom of the ad was a logo for Minitel.

Minitel. The machine that seemed like a glimpse into the future when it first appeared. The man knew what it was. Everyone in the city did. There was a time, not long ago, when the plastic terminals started showing up across the city. No longer just in homes, where the telephone company provided a small, boxy screen and a keyboard connected to the Minitel servers through the phone lines. Larger versions started appearing in the lobbies of train stations and shopping malls. *Minitel was the future,* they had said. A French marvel, ahead of the rest of the world. You didn't need to buy a newspaper to check the headlines anymore. You didn't need to pick up the phone to book a train ticket or call an operator to look up an address. You didn't need to post a letter to write to someone far away. You only had to type in a numeric code, and all would be on the screen. 36.11 for the phone book. 36.15 for private paid services.

At least, that was the idea.

The man had used one a few times, back when the excitement of Minitel was still fresh, back when people *wanted* to believe in it. But it was something that drained your francs, minute by minute, while you stared at its pixelated text. Some places on the Minitel servers were practical and free, job listings, travel information. Other more personal rooms were charged: chat lines, lonely hearts ads, secret places where people sent messages into the void, hoping anyone would answer.

And now, as he saw on the billboard, Santa Claus had his own Minitel chat room. A digital Father Christmas, that had a charge to speak to.

Maybe it was some department store gimmick. A digitized toy catalogue, where children could beg their parents to type in the code and browse pages of gifts they could never afford. Or perhaps it was some novelty, where, for a few centimes, a machine would spit out pre-written words from Santa, filled with empty yet festive cheer.

Or... *maybe*, the man thought... Maybe it was real. Maybe Santa Claus wasn't in the North Pole at all. Maybe he had simply moved with the times. Swapped chimneys for the telephone lines. What better way to reach children? What better way to speak to them... through Minitel. Through the future.

The wind picked up slightly, tugging at the wool of the man's bright yellow scarf. He stood for a moment longer, longingly looking at the image of Santa, before finally moving on, leaving not only the smashed snow globe on the ground, but also any hope that he would find someone who would play with him.

Was it because he had no home that people walked away at the sight of him? Was it his face? Was he not a nice-looking man? He did not know the answer, as if he did know he would change it.

The snow began to fall on the streets once more, as the chill returned to his fingers.

In the dining room of the manor house, daylight spilled in across the long oak table. The room was stately, yet tired, just like the rest of the house. The silver was slightly tarnished, the wallpaper faded at the seams. It was homely yet not pristine.

Julie sat at her usual chair, flipping through the business pages of the newspaper.

A cup of coffee sat cold at her elbow. A cup she had completely forgotten about.

Thomas walked in, dragging his grandfather by his handcuffed wrist.

"Mom, I captured a half-blind, diabetic soldier behind enemy lines," he announced. "You should give me a medal."

Julie didn't need to look up to know what was going on. "Thomas, that's your grandfather. Show him a little respect, please."

"It's okay, Julie," Papy shrugged, with a smile. "He's right... I *am* a half-blind and diabetic soldier."

He leaned down to kiss her good morning, but as he tried, he was tugged away, with Thomas pulling him to the other side of the table.

A maid entered, Linda, with a tray in hand. She set down a fresh cup of coffee beside Julie, taking away the cold one. Julie nodded in thanks.

"Morning Linda!" Thomas said to the maid with a wide grin. A polar opposite attitude from the one his mother had.

"Hello there young Thomas," Linda replied, not missing a beat as she walked back into the kitchen.

Papy shuffled along the table, where his hand soon found the back of his chair.

"Julie, where are my pills?" he asked, sitting down as he still yawned away his sleep.

"They're right in front of you, Dad," Julie replied, eyes remaining fixed on the newspaper.

Papy's hands fumbled at the cup that sat on his placemat. A cup carrying half a dozen pills for him to swallow. Through his eyes, the world was a blur of indistinct shapes. He squinted as he tried to determine where his cup was.

"Right in front of you, Grandpa," Thomas said gently, reaching forward and sliding the cup nearer.

"Oh right, yes. I see them now," Papy lied, managing to grab the cup by sheer coincidence. "Just got a little bit distracted, that's all. I think I may be still asleep."

Thomas pointed at a breadbasket next to his mother. "Mom, can you pass a croissant?"

"You know the deal," Julie said, looking up at him with a smile. "First, *you* have to take your medication as well."

With a grimace, Thomas glared at the small glass of cough syrup in front of him. One he had been ignoring.

"Do I *have* to?" he moaned.

Papy smiled. "Say, you're not going to let me take medication all on my own, are you, Thommy?" he lifted his glass and a handful of pills. "Come on. Fastest one wins... Okay? On three... Bottom's up!"

Thomas, never one to miss a game, quickly picked up his syrup. He clinked the glass against his grandfather's.

"One... Two..." Papy started.

"Three!" Thomas interrupted as he started to drink his medicine as quick as he could.

Papy joined with swallowing his pills and drinking his water, but the handcuffs between them made it awkward, forcing them to move closer together in order to raise their glasses. Neither realizing they could just as easily use their other hands.

Julie watched them with an amused smile.

When finished, Thomas looked over to his mother expectantly.

"A deal's a deal," she shrugged, picking up a croissant and tossing it across the table to him.

Thomas caught it easily and, without hesitation, took a big bite from one end.

"How are you, my dear?" Papy said, turning to his daughter. "Will it be a busy day at the store today?"

"No more than usual." She said, then motioned to her newspaper. "I saw that shares of the Toy Center are down. What do you think, Dad? Should I buy it?"

"You don't think you already own enough?"

Julie laughed. "Never!"

"Oh yeah, Mom, buy more stores!" Thomas said enthusiastically between bites. "Then I'll have even more toys."

"What? You don't have enough already?" Julie replied, raising an eyebrow.

"You don't understand," Thomas said eagerly. "If I get more, I can sell them back to Santa, and get rich!"

Papy chuckled. "He's his mother's son, that's for sure."

Julie hesitated, then said quietly, "More like his father than me..."

Thomas' smile faltered as her words landed.

Grandpa, unaware of the shift in mood, added cheerfully, "Of course, just like his father."

Julie noticed her son's expression, but before she could speak, Thomas quickly changed the subject, forcing a smile once more.

"Pilou says Santa doesn't exist. Says it's the parents who give the presents..."

"Pilou?" Papy scoffed. "That kid's crazy. What does he know?"

Julie put her newspaper down. "No, no, Pilou is totally right."

Both Thomas and Papy turned to her, somewhat shocked.

"For *him*," she continued, "Santa Claus doesn't exist at all. Pilou is on the naughty list. He's bad at school, rude to his parents... so, Santa doesn't come to his house. On Christmas Eve, *if* he gets any gifts, it's because his parents have given them to him. So for him, Santa doesn't exist at all. But for you, it's a different matter. You're not naughty."

Thomas chewed thoughtfully. "That makes sense, I guess." And just like any child his age, his thoughts then switched again. "Oh, you hear that there's a new way to send letters to Santa now? You see that?"

"A new way?"

"Yeah, you can send him a letter by Minitel."

Julie hesitated, glancing at her father, who just looked confused. "By Minitel? That computer thing?" she said. "Well... I'm not sure computers are something Santa would use... If I were you, I'd just write a letter. It's much safer."

"I did that already!" Thomas exclaimed proudly, producing a small envelope from his pocket. "I wrote it last night. Can you mail it for me?"

Passing the envelope to Papy, the old man handed it to Julie, who slipped it into her suit jacket.

A sharp honk from outside shattered their morning, washing over Thomas with a wave of irritation.

Julie tensed visibly as she got up from the table and walked around to her son's seat. Without a word they exchanged a complicated, secret handshake, made up of slaps of palms and clicks of fingers.

"No experiments today, okay?" she asked. "We can't have more holes in the floor. The house is starting to look like Swiss cheese."

Thomas took her hand on the last shake and kissed it like a knight.

"I'll take that as a yes," she said. "Now, Thomas,

you are in charge today, okay? Don't forget Papy's insulin, okay? You remember how it's all done?"

"Of course!"

"Water is just as good, you know?" Papy complained, half-joking. "All this medicine is useless."

Julie shook her head as she walked to the door, picking her coat off a stand. "Oh and I've got an important meeting tonight. So, I'll be back a bit later than usual."

As soon as the front door clicked shut behind her, Thomas stood up, with a frown.

Though he did not get far, as the toy handcuffs still bound him to his grandfather's wrist. With a sharp tug, the plastic chain came loose, and he tossed the cuffs aside, not wanting to play anymore.

Outside, waiting at the bottom of the drive was a metallic gray Porsche. Its engine rumbled as the windshield wipers wiped the snow away in a constant rhythm.

Julie, with her scarf tucked tightly around her neck, walked down the steps and across the pebbled drive.

As she passed the hedges, Charles the

groundskeeper looked up from where he was clearing snow along the path.

"Morning, Ma'am," he said.

Julie smiled. "Hello, Charles. Are you having a nice morning?" She didn't wait for an answer. She just asked out of politeness, not interest, and Charles knew that, so he didn't even attempt a reply.

She got into the waiting car and closed the door behind her.

From the driver's seat, Roland leaned nearer to Julie. The collar of his expensive wool coat brushed her cheek as he attempted to steal a kiss. But Julie, offering nothing but a glance and a thin smile, turned her head away and looked out of the window.

"Not here," she said firmly. "Let's just go, okay?"

Roland didn't protest. He just sat back with an understanding smile and put the car into gear.

The vehicle moved forward on the gravel, pulling away from the manor house as they sat in silence.

High above, behind a second-floor window, Thomas watched out sadly. His breath fogged the pane as he saw the car disappear beyond the trees.

CHAPTER TWO

Now that the clock struck 9am, the city was almost fully awake.

The department store had sat like an empty hive waiting for its swarm to return. Its wide glass windows displayed tidy empty rows of products beneath strips of fluorescent lighting that remained lit all night.

When the opening hour hit, and the doors were unlocked, the swarm had been queuing outside, and filled the store in an instant. It was abuzz with consumerism within a few moments, especially with it being the day before Christmas eve.

In the quieter administrative wing, where the public could not enter, the corridors ran long and narrow, separating office after office.

Julie stepped out from the elevator first, her heels clacking on the freshly waxed floor. Roland followed her, with a thick folder in his hand. They cut through to a conference room at one end.

"We have to go all out this year," she said without looking at him. "Thomas won't believe in Santa Claus for much longer."

"He's turning ten. It's normal for him to see the truth, isn't it?" Roland said as he handed her a document resting on the folder, along with a pen.

Julie took them, signed the paper on the move, on autopilot as she continued. "So what if he's ten? I believed until I was thirteen. So, I'm gonna make sure he believes as long as possible."

Roland smirked. "Thirteen? But you weren't a prodigy like he is."

He barely got the words out before she shot him a warning glance. She stopped walking.

He almost stuttered as he added quickly. "You didn't spend every weekend inventing software, building things, did you? That kid is beyond smart."

"Thomas isn't like *that*, he's just creative," she said. Then, defensively, "And how would you know anyway?"

Roland didn't know what to say, he just stared back.

She then let out a heavy sigh. "Okay. Fine. Yes,

he's... very intelligent. More than I was... But that doesn't mean he can't believe in things like this. Or in fairies or elves or anything else magical. He may be a whizz at computers... or even cutting holes in the floor... But that's what's beautiful about him. He's still just a child. He still has that wonder."

"Cutting holes in the floor?" Roland asked.

She reached into her coat pocket and pulled out a folded letter. "Here, if you want proof, look at this. Can you see the address?"

Roland looked at it, reading aloud with an amused smile, "Santa Claus, the North Pole." He laughed, shaking his head. "Okay, leave it with me. I'll get him a load of awesome things, okay? I'll get them sent to the groundkeeper as usual."

They reached the door to the conference room. Julie raised a hand, but before she could push open the door, Roland caught her by the wrist. His voice dropped to an almost whisper.

"Will I see you later?"

Her eyes met his. She didn't answer. Just smiled, mischievous and noncommittal.

The conference room was lined with two things: suits and tension. All men, all already on their feet the moment Julie stepped inside. Her presence was their cue.

She waved a hand. "Sit down, gentlemen. Please."

She took her seat at the head of the long glass table, dropped her bag beside her, and got straight into the meeting.

"I called this for one reason. As you know, tomorrow is Christmas Eve. So for that reason, we'll be open late as expected."

A few heads tilted. Murmurs rippled across the table. She pressed on, unbothered.

"We're hiring extra staff immediately. I put a call out through HR to find show people. I asked for roller-skating fairies. Fire-eaters. Clowns. We'll dress the cashiers in costume. Full make-up."

The murmurs soon shifted to groans. One of the men coughed pointedly. Another exhaled hard.

Julie continued, not missing a beat. "And I want Santas on every corner. Real Santas. Not ones with wristwatches or trousers below their robes. I want joy. I want a celebration. A party. I want it to be absolutely clear to all children that Santa Claus shops with us."

A man near the middle raised a hand. He didn't wait to be called.

"But..." he began, "a celebration like that takes planning, not just getting people hired. There's no time. Why didn't we talk about this a month ago?"

Julie met his gaze. Calm. Unflinching.

"Because a month ago," she said, "I thought that children still believed in Santa Claus, but have you seen out there? At the other stores? There is no celebration of the season at all. Just lots of decoration. We need to bring the joy back. The wonder. The spectacle. We need to be the one place people equate to the season. Printemps equals Christmas. You understand?"

Sitting on the floor of Thomas' bedroom, the Minitel screen blinked with an electric hum as it whirred to life.

The cold sunlight filtered in through the closed curtains, casting a weak glow over piles of discarded candy wrappers and scattered toys. Thomas sat cross-legged, a half-finished lollipop in his mouth, as he typed into the Minitel keyboard.

Beside him was his friend, Pilou, twelve and heavily freckled. He was now of the age where he was perpetually unimpressed with everything in life. He grabbed a handful of jellybeans from a bowl, and shoved them into his mouth while staring at the glowing computer with growing contempt.

"You don't see it do you?" Pilou scoffed. "They just keep asking the same dumb questions: What's your name? How old are you? Have you been good this year?" He took another handful of jellybeans. "This thing's for idiots."

Thomas didn't look up from the screen as he typed. "*You're* the idiot," he muttered. "You don't believe in *anything*."

Pilou leaned back against the side of the bed, with a smile. "Yeah? And you believe in *everything*. I already told you, Santa doesn't exist. He's not real. He's a stupid lie." He pointed at the screen. "Look. It's starting again."

On the Minitel was the holding screen of the chat room they had entered: 3615 Code Santa Claus. At the bottom, words blinked into view:

WHAT'S YOUR NAME?

"There," Pilou said feeling triumphant. "Same as before. Same as it always is."

Thomas leaned in, getting defensive. "That's only because he's not there right now. This is a program, like a... a... like an answering machine or something. That's all."

Pilou snorted. "An answering machine? Really? You wanna talk to an answering machine now?"

"I'm telling you, he'll reply when he gets the message, you'll see."

Thomas then spoke to himself, dictating the words as his fingers typed.

"My name is Thomas... Santa, if you are real... please answer."

The screen flickered and a new message came up:

WHAT'S YOUR AGE?

"I'm out," Pilou groaned. "I've had enough of this."

He got to his feet, brushing the candy remnants from his jeans, and picked up his puffy winter coat from the bed. He put it on and zipped it up.

Thomas didn't even look up as he was fixed to the screen. "Yeah, fine, go. Get lost! I don't want you here you anyway!"

"You're seriously stupid, Thomas" Pilou mumbled, already halfway to the door. "You gotta stop acting like a baby."

Thomas raised his voice so Pilou could hear him as he left the room. "Well, this stupid kid won't help you with your homework." He grimaced as he turned angrily to the now-empty door. "And if your video games break again?" he shouted. "Don't come crying to me!"

With a loud, exaggerated sight—sounding just like his mother—he turned back to the screen, but something on there had changed.

A new message had been written on there. Not a prewritten one.

This is Santa Claus, What can I do
for you, Thomas?

Thomas' heart skipped a beat. *"Pilou!"* he
shrieked. "Come back! He answered! Santa actually
answered!"

His fingers hit the keyboard, jittery with
excitement as he typed.

So you DO exist!

The response came quickly.

I hope I do, or I wouldn't be able
to type this! Ha Ha!

Pilou reappeared, breathless, the coat half-
unzipped. "If this is some kind of joke, I swear I'll
beat your ass."

Thomas pointed at the screen with wide eyes.
"Look! See for yourself."

Pilou dropped back onto the floor, hesitated for a
second, then reached for the jellybean bowl and
helped himself to another handful, as if nothing had
just happened between them.

Thomas typed, narrating loudly as he did:
"Where do you live?"

The terminal paused, then came its reply:

In the North Pole, of course.

Pilou laughed through a mouthful of candy.
"Okay, this guy's just some jerk."

"You're the jerk."

Pilou turned serious again. "Don't you see? He's just saying whatever you want to hear. Just 'cause he says he is Santa, doesn't make him Santa, you know that don't you?"

Thomas didn't answer, he just looked at the messages on screen.

"Here," Pilou added." Let me ask him something."

Thomas shrugged with a nod, fingers over the keyboard, waiting for the question.

"Ask him," Pilou said, "if he *really* has elves working for him, like in the stories. Get him to describe them. I wanna see what he comes up with. 'Cause in the stories the elves are either little creatures or little people. We gotta get him to say details... Details are where liars slip up!"

The jellybeans were eaten loudly between Pilou's teeth as Thomas typed the question.

No, came the reply.

Pilou sat back, surprised at the reply. "Huh. I thought for sure he'd say yes to that... Can't find a lie if he just says no."

Thomas laughed. "That's because your question was dumb."

He typed again, speaking aloud with each word: "Are you coming to my house tomorrow night?"

A long pause. Then:

Why do you ask if you already know
the answer?

Thomas typed fast. "To see if you're the real Santa Claus, of course."

The screen refreshed as the new words appeared at the top of the screen.

I am the <u>only</u> Santa Claus. If you
don't believe me, then I will go now.
Belief is everything.

Thomas hurriedly tapped the keyboard. "Don't get mad. I believe you!"

Do you want to play a game?

Pilou shifted uneasily at this latest question. "You should stop talking to this guy. Seriously... This isn't right. You're not talking to Santa..." he sighed. "*Do you want to play a game?* That's his question? Really? You're probably connected to the wrong server or something. One for perverts and weirdos..."

Thomas ignored the comment, before going back to typing. "What do you want to play?"

Deep in the belly of the Christmas rush of panic buyers, people scurried through the train station concourse. Loudspeaker announcements loudly sounded off the tiled walls and echoed into a shuffle of suitcases, shoes and expectant commerce.

Tucked in one of the shadowed corners stood a large, public Minitel terminal. Made of a cheap gray plastic, it appeared to be concrete. Over the Minitel's keyboard, a man in a bright yellow scarf was typing. His eyes were wide as they stared at the flickering text on the screen.

`Do you want to play a game?` he typed.

The reply came:

`What do you want to play?`

He smiled as he typed his reply: `Will you give me your address?`

The reply took a few uncomfortable seconds to come.

`But you already know my address! You're Santa, you see everything!`

The man paused. Not knowing what to reply, as the message from Thomas continued.

`Did you want my letter? I gave it to my mom. She has it. You can go get it from her store. She's the manager at Printemps. Lots of great toys there to bring to me!`

The man looked around. Not knowing what to do now. All he wanted was someone to play with. But this question confused him as he was caught in a lie.

Before he could type a reply, the Minitel screen

refreshed to the home screen, as the chat room connection ended, with his credits running out.

Deposit your coins to continue...

"No," the man whispered. "No, no, no..."

He hurriedly fumbled in his coat pockets and pulled out a few old coins. Quickly feeding them into the slot, he grunted loudly as the machine rejected them out of the return slot.

"No!" he shouted. Slamming his hand on the screen in a sudden rage. He jabbed at the keys, harder. But the session had ended.

The welcome screen to the chat room reappeared, its bold text, like it was taunting him: **3615 CODE SANTA CLAUS.**

He looked unblinking and trying to suppress his anger. He had a new friend, and now this machine had stolen him away.

Slowly, his grimace fell away as he remembered what the boy said. His mother was the manager of Printemps. He nodded to himself and stepped back, disappearing into the blur of the crowd milling behind him.

The snow was falling again after a short respite, flitting gently across the people that had formed outside the glass-fronted entrance of the department store. Beneath the bold signage that read *Printemps*, warmly dressed shoppers gathered, waiting to get in through the masses of shoppers ahead of them. Children pointed at toys in the windows, as parents shuffled, bored and cold, having to get through this as fast as they could.

Among them, he stood—the man with the bright yellow scarf. He moved slowly, looking cautiously around. The crowd was making him nervous. Unlike the others, he did not look at the windows, nor the decorations, but at the people. His gaze soon fell upon a man dressed in a basic Santa costume. A red-suit, white, fake beard, smiling for photos and crouching to accept the embraces of eager children. The crowd here adored him. The children laughed at his jokes.

But the man in the scarf didn't smile. He just stared. They loved this man, despite his looking like a cheap knockoff.

Walking on, the man noticed a paper sign across the top of the entrance to the store. It flapped slightly in the wind: *We are hiring for the holidays!*

He read it. Then read it again.

He stared around to the cheap Santa once more, then walked into the store.

Through the glass doors, the warmth inside hit like a wall. The usual department store muzak played overhead, as the scents of perfume, makeup counters, and roasted chestnuts from a foot stall vendor hit him even harder. Everything here was a sensory overload. He knew he did not belong in this building, among these people, yet he forced himself to move on anyway.

Walking up to a large information desk, he smiled his best smile at the receptionist.

"You need someone?" he muttered. "The sign outside?"

The woman looked him up and down, over his dirty coat and tangled brown beard, and without thinking any more of it, pointed him to a hallway off to the left.

Within minutes, he found himself seated at a desk in one of the store's offices. An employment form lay in front of him.

Pen in hand, he leaned forward to fill it out. His writing was like a child's as he answered each question slow and uncertain, afraid of making a single mistake.

When it came to the address section, he couldn't tell the truth: that he had no home and slept wherever was warm. Instead, he wrote down the orphanage where he'd grown up. It wasn't a lie, not exactly. It was a place he had once lived, just not where he lived now.

They had explained to him that this was all last-minute. Work would start today and last until the end of Boxing Day. It seemed they didn't care much who they hired, only that someone filled the role. They were looking for clowns to juggle, elves to hand out gifts, performers of any kind to make the store a festive celebration, but he knew what he wanted to do.

And they were more than happy to say yes.

When he had finished filling out his details, a woman returned. There was no questions, no small talk. Just a plastic hanger. On it hung a red robe and a white fake beard.

The manor sat beneath the setting sun, its windows dark, save for two glowing panes on its highest floor: the attic.

Inside, the light from a series of monitors cast a blue hue over the cluttered room. Wires littered the desk, attached across a dozen circuit boards, as diodes across them flashed.

Thomas was hunched over them, soldering iron in hand, wearing protective glasses that caught the reflections from the monitors, as he attached the last wire to its place.

With one hand, he reached over to the keyboard

and typed quickly, keeping his eyes on all the screens. One showed a never-ending scroll of computer code. Another displayed wireframe designs of each room in the house, and the last showed the manor's top-down blueprint. Glowing red points flashed across the screen. Each point signified something in the house that he had installed and attached to this array. Motion sensors. Traps. Cameras. All flashed red, and were all online.

J.R. lay on the floor nearby, watching with uncomprehending attention.

"System's ready," Thomas said, not to the dog but out loud to the room. "Now I gotta configure the link between the monitor, traps, and cameras..."

He turned to the dog, reached over and scratched behind the dog's ear.

"This is a big moment, J.R." he said, happily. "This is zero hour."

The dog got excited, jumped up, tail wagging, and immediately tried to lick Thomas' face.

"No, not now!" Thomas laughed. "You can see that I'm working!"

He gently pushed the dog aside, and turned back to the screens.

"Okay," he said, thinking aloud once more. "System check function sequence..."

He tapped a few keys, and the program

launched, only for the screen to start stuttering. The lines of code on the screen quickly began to repeat the same line, over and over.

"Damn. Why is it looping?" he muttered.

As he hit the commands on the keyboard, the code stopped scrolling.

Then it hit him. He snapped his fingers. "Of course. I forgot to reset the index on the matrix." His expression then dropped. "Back to square one then, genius."

With a fresh set of keystrokes, he began again. And within five minutes, the code had been rewritten.

"Launching compile sequence."

He sat still. Waiting.

The system whirred. A soft chime. Then:

NO ERROR FOUND.

LINK ESTABLISHED.

Thomas leaned back, grinning happily. "And one quick assembler call to optimize..."

He typed in a last command, then picked up an armband monitor. A plastic gauntlet that strapped over his forearm. With a small screen on it, and a dozen switches and buttons, it was his main controller for all the devices he had linked.

When it was strapped on, the small screen lit up.

The feed from one of the cameras filled the black and white low-resolution display.

He laughed, triumphantly. "We did it, J.R. We won! Do you see this?"

The dog barked once, wagging his tail, not understanding but reacting to Thomas' enthusiasm.

"With this, I can monitor all my traps, every room... I can record all my camera feeds! And if Santa's real... *really* real... then tomorrow night I'll see him with my own eyes. And I'll have proof. Proof I can show the world. And maybe..."

He paused.

"Maybe I'll even catch him."

In his apartment in the middle of downtown, Roland sat shirtless against the pillows. The sheets were warm as Julie stood at the foot of the bed, her blouse gone, as her skirt fell around her calves. Stepping forward, now only in her underwear, she climbed over the bed hungrily toward him.

Roland reached for her. His fingers slipped under one bra strap, then the other, undid the clasp until it came loose and she shrugged it off.

He cupped her neck, pulled her to him, and they kissed. His hand began to move lower. As his fingertips touched the elastic of her knickers—

The phone rang.

Julie murmured against his skin, lips by his ear. "Let it ring…"

The phone continued, relentlessly.

"It *might* be important," he said.

Julie silenced him with another kiss, pulling him back down into the mattress.

"Nothing's *that* important."

Still kissing, Roland fumbled blindly for the phone that sat on the nightstand. He soon found the receiver.

'Hello' A boy's voice said. '*Can I speak to my mother, please?*'

Roland shot up. "Wh-who is this?"

'*It's Thomas de Frémont. Can you put my mother on the phone?*'

Hearing his voice, Julie stopped, her romantic moment vanishing in a breath.

Roland was already panicking. "Thomas? Uh… this is Roland. Your mother isn't… she's not…"

'*Not there?*' Thomas said. '*I see. I'll try the office next. Thank you. Goodbye, sir.*'

Click. The line went dead.

Roland lowered the receiver slowly. "He knows," he whispered.

Julie didn't speak.

Roland continued. "He *knows*. And he knows that I know he knows!"

Julie quickly got out of bed, and started to dress in silence, with an unreadable expression.

Roland turned his gaze to the ceiling, jaw clenched. Maybe she was right to keep him out of it. Maybe he was just a complication. But something in him burned. Not jealousy, not pride, just the hollow certainty that she would never let him mean anything to that boy.

"You know what I think, Julie? I think he *wants* to know me."

"No. He does not." She replied in a monotone. "Trust me."

"Maybe, maybe not. Either way, I would like to know him. But you, you won't let it happen... You and I have been together long enough, and you've hidden it all. You've built these walls, these compartments that keep me away from your home life."

Julie, mostly dressed, grabbed her bag and without a word, walked out the door.

In the manor's garage, a single bulb hung above a dusty and faded 1980 Ford Taunus. Lifted on a jack, its bonnet was also up.

Thomas lay on his back, lying on a skateboard beneath the car. He wore overalls that were several sizes too big. The sleeves of which were rolled up and the legs bunched at the knees. With a headlamp strapped to his forehead, its beam shone upon where he worked with spanners on the underbelly of the vehicle. Only his shoes stuck out from under the chassis.

Papy sat nearby on a stool, a toolbox balanced on his lap. His hands fumbled through the clutter of metal, trying to distinguish each tool by feel as his eyesight could not distinguish the small numbers and letters on each.

"This car is so old," Thomas called out from beneath the car. "Why doesn't Mom just get a Testarossa or something cool like that?"

Papy gave a shrug. "Sentimental reasons. She cares about this car. Always has."

"Well, it's definitely weird," Thomas said. "She can afford a much better one."

"Weird?" Papy echoed with amusement. "Or maybe just... special. It is the car she met your father in."

Thomas stopped for a second. Then he reached a hand outward, fingers clicking. "Twelve-millimetre wrench, please!"

"Pardon?"

Thomas raised his voice so his grandfather could hear better. "Twelve-millimetre wrench, please."

Papy leaned forward, eyes narrowing. "It's murder trying to read the numbers on these things, you know. I mean, I *can* see, obviously, but not exactly clearly."

He brought a wrench up close, squinting at it from just a few inches away. In his field of vision, the number was a blur.

"Twelve, you said?"

"Yes, please."

Papy fumbled through the tools, finally offering one at random that looked like it might fit the bill.

By chance, it was the right one.

"Thanks, Papy."

Thomas continued his work. After a few solid turns of the bolt, he emerged, the skateboard rolling out with him. His face and hands were streaked with grease.

"That should hold it for now," he said, wiping his face with the back of his sleeve. He got to his feet, picked up the skateboard and laid it carefully on the workbench.

"Can you take the wheel, Papy?"

"Sure thing, what should I do?"

"Just turn it on when I say."

Papy nodded as he slowly stood up and walked

over to the car, shuffling himself over to the driver's side door.

Thomas crouched beside the front wheel and wound down the jack that had been holding the car up.

When it was on the ground, Papy got behind the wheel.

"Wait for me to tell you to turn it on," Thomas said, reaching under the hood.

"Of course," came the reply from the driver's seat.

After a few checks, Thomas nodded to himself.

"Okay. Go!"

The ignition clicked. The engine wheezed, coughed, but didn't catch.

"Hold on!" Thomas said, as he reached inside once more and adjusted the throttle cable.

"Now keep the key turned, but don't pump the gas"

A second later, Papy turned the key, and the engine quickly roared to life.

Both let out a cheer.

"Yeah!" Thomas beamed. "Now give it a rev!"

Papy tapped the accelerator, and the engine purred louder. Thomas slammed the hood closed with satisfaction and walked around to the driver's side, wiping his hands on his overalls.

"My turn!" Thomas said, opening the driver's side door.

"With pleasure," Papy replied, shifting over to the passenger side.

Thomas climbed in, barely able to reach the pedals. He adjusted the seat as far forward as it would go and held onto the wheel.

"We'll warm her up a bit," he said, pressing the accelerator gently.

Papy looked at his grandson, smiling. "You know, Tommy... I'm proud of you. And I think your Mom would be too, if she saw you right now. You do things that I could never have done. You're quite a genius."

Thomas looked over his shoulder as he put the car in reverse.

"Well, now I have this working, she won't need anyone to drive her to work anymore," he said, easing the car back out of the garage and onto the driveway.

The car spluttered then growled, as it found a rhythm, driving onto the garden's path.

Thomas was perched forward, peering over the wheel, as he put the car into drive.

"Wanna go around the house, Papy?" he asked, already turning the wheel before the old man could answer.

Papy gripped the handle above the door. "Yes, but take it easy, eh?" he said. "No weaving between the trees this time. And please, not too fast... My old bones don't like it."

"Of course!" Thomas replied, and with a smile that said he had no intention of doing either.

As he pressed down hard on the accelerator, the car shot forward. Its tires kicked up gravel and leaves as it zipped around the side of the building.

CHAPTER THREE

Thomas and his grandfather, both still in their pajamas, leaned over the twin basins in the bathroom. Their faces were covered in white shaving foam—thick on the cheeks, heavier around the chin.

Papy's hand dragged the razor across his jaw. His weak grip trembled, but he had done this enough times not to cut his skin. He squinted into the mirror, moving carefully though his blurred vision. His fingers felt their way across his face as he moved the razor, shaving more by memory than sight.

Thomas, on the other hand, was armed with a plastic toy knife, the kind that couldn't cut a thing. He mimicked his grandfather's movements with a focused intensity, dragging the plastic over his foam-covered skin as if performing a sacred ceremony.

Julie appeared in the doorway behind them,

dressed for work in her suit. She took in the scene with a weary sigh.

"I *told* you to wait for me, dad," she said, stepping into the room. "You'll end up cutting yourself."

Papy snorted, unconcerned. "Bah. This isn't baby skin. It's like leather! When is the last time I cut myself, huh?"

Julie shook her head but smiled as she gently pried the razor from his hand. "All the more reason to be careful," she said. "Leather is expensive, and you don't ever want to cut it."

He didn't protest as she guided him onto the small-cushioned stool beside the sink. With slow strokes of the brush, she re-lathered his face . Then she took the blade and began to shave. Long steady lines around his jawline, washing the edge of the razor under the warm water between each pass.

At the other sink, Thomas continued his own performance, watching them in the mirror.

"You know," he said, scraping his toy knife across his top lip, "with Minitel, you don't just order presents. You can talk to Santa."

Julie didn't answer. Her expression remained unchanged; she gave no indication of hearing. Not a flinch, not a twitch. She simply kept shaving.

"Did you hear me?" Thomas asked.

"Yes," Julie replied. "You told us about Minitel yesterday, remember?"

Thomas frowned slightly, then changed tack.

"It's nice, isn't it? Us, like this. All three of us, together."

Julie paused mid-shave. "What's *that* supposed to mean?"

"Just that I don't see you much. I miss you, that's all."

She froze for a second, then resumed shaving, knowing where this was going. More passive aggressive barbs.

"Are you coming home early?" Thomas asked. "Or you got another one of those 'important meetings'?"

Julie finished shaving her father, then set the razor down on the sink, picked up a cloth, and began wiping away the remaining foam from her father's chin. Then she turned, with a calm, but very stern voice. "Listen to me, Thomas. I need you to stop interrogating me all the time. Stop watching everything I do. I am very busy and have so much to do. You need to stop spying on me like you're—"

"I'm *not* spying on you!" he shot back.

"No? Then why did you call up last Ronald night? There was no emergency. No reason at all to interrupt any business."

Thomas looked to his feet, feeling guilty.

"You cannot just expect me to be at your beck and call 24/7. I run a department store, and Christmas is our busiest time. If I don't run it well, we don't make money. If we don't make money, we can't afford to run this house. Do you understand?"

Julie looked at him for a long moment, then, without a word, dropped the cloth onto the sink then left the room.

She soon left for work without saying goodbye.

She hadn't wanted Roland to pick her up. She didn't want the chatter, the questions, the kiss he always tried to steal. She needed silence. Needed the cold morning air. Needed time to think.

At the end of the drive, waiting for her, sat a dark-windowed executive taxi. She decided against taking the car that Thomas fixed, not because she didn't trust his work, but it was not a car the CEO of a company should turn up to work in.

As she got in, she could not help but think of how Thomas might react if she ever introduced Roland as her boyfriend. No man would ever be enough for her son to accept. Not after what happened. Not after what he saw.

How do you introduce someone new when your child has already watched the man he adored bleed out on the dining room floor?

Julie sat quietly as the taxi drove off, sad at what Thomas had seen. She closed her eyes, as if it could push the worry back down into the recesses of her mind. But it was always there, waiting beneath the surface.

The night of the break-in, she had been working late as usual. Her husband had gotten home early to put the five-year-old Thomas to bed.

As he slept, Thomas did not hear the smash of glass downstairs. He did not hear his father's angry words nor threats to the intruders who broke in to ransack the manor. He did not even hear the shouts or fighting that ensued.

But Thomas *did* hear the gunshot.

Thomas had heard it loud and clear.

Woken, he crept out of bed, and walked downstairs to see what the noise was. And he walked straight into a nightmare.

He saw his father. Barely alive. Eyes still open. Struggling to breathe to speak to the terrified Thomas. Spluttering that he loved him, and to not be afraid.

The men who committed the crime had fled after the gunshot, and they were caught within hours. Then arrested, named, and subsequently jailed for life. But that justice didn't bring peace. Not for her and not for Thomas.

Since that night, he hadn't been the same. He grew up fast over the next few years. Intent on keeping the manor safe.

He had wired the building like a fortress. Covered every room he could with cameras. Built traps into the walls and floors, as if trying to undo what had already been done.

He called it preparation.

Julie called it grief.

And she let him do exactly what he wanted, because how do you say no to a boy who's just trying to feel safe? How do you deny him the only comfort he had left?

So she didn't. She gave him total freedom. She gave him space. She gave him silence. Because love, sometimes, is knowing when not to say a word.

Now, though, her life was unable to move on. Roland was not a possibility as long as Thomas would be hurt by it. But now his snips and badgering were getting too much.

Later that day, outside the department store, the snow had already drawn its curtain across the city. But that had deterred no one. On the streets, the crowd was out in abundance, thick and noisy in front of the store's bright lights. Children's voices shrieked and overlapped like birds, as their excitement mounted, watching the dozen or so performers fanned out around the edges of the building.

Fire-breathers blew arcs of flame into the air, as clowns darted among the children, making balloon animals and juggling balls. A contortionist tied themselves in a knot on a small plinth. A group of carollers sang loudly. A fairy on roller skates twirled past the glass entrance, her wand catching the light with every spin, making the children marvel at her grace. It didn't matter if the kids believed in these festivities; the spectacle Printemps had put on, even at such a last minute, was something to behold. One could not help but get dragged into the celebratory mood in its presence.

A short clown shouted through a megaphone at the crowd, ushering them into the store. "Today, we have such a spectacle for you to see! Ladies, gentlemen, children of all ages, witness Christmas... Printemps style! Enjoy yourselves as you shop! We have acrobats, jugglers and all manner of magic! And I myself, will entertain you with my terrible gymnastic feats! So come and laugh with us, buy your presents and have a merry, merry Christmas!"

In the middle of it all, seated in an elaborate sleigh trimmed with cotton wool snow, was a man in a Santa Claus costume. Children crowded near, climbing up onto the sleigh's small wooden steps, hesitating by the velvet ropes until it was their turn to see the man of the hour.

But this Santa wasn't like any of the others in the city.

This one watched the children too closely. His eyes looked, lingering. His fingers twitched when a child brushed too near. He did not think malevolent thoughts, though. He only thought one thing: maybe some of these children would want to play with him. Not run away as they usually did. Not scream like some. Not force him to lose his temper...

Under his costume, a bright yellow scarf poked out from the neckline.

A girl stepped up, looking at him like he was magic. She wore no scarf, and her coat was buttoned a little crookedly, as if she had done it up herself. There were no parents beside her, she was alone.

He leaned forward and beckoned her to come closer, which she happily did. Picking her up he placed her on his lap and stared at her with a wide smile.

Was this his new friend? He thought. He hoped so. He really hoped so. His white gloved hand stroked her face, but as it did, her smile faltered slightly.

"What's your name?" he asked, his voice soft and sweet.

"Marion," she replied unsure.

Her expression showed a growing worry as the man continued to stroke her face. But to him, he was just being friendly. He was just being jolly. He brushed her cheek once more.

Marion squirmed, not liking it one bit.

"I don't like your face," she said, staring right into his eyes.

As he heard it, his hand and his smile dropped.

"You're *not* the real Santa," she added.

She reached up without hesitation and tugged at his fake beard. It came loose with one yank, revealing his full, stunned expression beneath.

It was only a second, but the pause before what happened was one of abject horror for the man. A damning insult. She didn't like his face? Why? What had he done? He just wanted to be her friend.

Then came the slap.

Sharp, fast, and full of rage. A slap he could not hold back as he hit Marion across the cheek.

The sound echoed around them as the girl fell backwards.

Instantly, Julie appeared, having just arrived at work. She snatched Marion up into her arms, and pulled her away from the man.

"What are you *doing?*" she snapped at him. "Are you crazy? You can't hit a child!"

The man's eyes, so soft before, now burned at the child and her.

Julie looked around. Thankfully, no one seemed to have noticed. Not yet anyway. The crowd in front of the store slowly moved on, distracted by the fire-breathers and the other revelling noise. She wrapped her arms tighter around the now crying girl, and pulled her away.

"There, there, don't cry, sweetheart," she murmured. "It's alright. Where's your mother?"

"She went in to buy something," Marion blubbed. "Said she'd only be five minutes."

"She left you all alone?"

"Not alone. She left me with Santa."

Julie glanced over her shoulder at the man still sitting in the sleigh, his fake white beard now hanging awkwardly from one ear. She lowered her voice to the child.

"We'll wait for her together, alright?"

She then turned to the man: "You don't know me, but I am the manager of this store, and you are *fired*. Go to the HR office *now*. And consider yourself lucky I don't call the police."

She turned away, walking through the crowd with Marion close by her side.

The door to the Human Resources office was closed.

The yellow scarfed man stepped up to it, still in his Santa costume. He shook nervously as he weakly knocked on the glass. Without waiting for a reply he walked inside.

The room was sterile. There was no celebration, laughter, or warmth in here like there was outside. Here, it was just white walls and metal desks.

"One moment please!" a voice shouted from behind a desk, currently in mid-conversation on the phone. It was the head of Human Resources. Roland.

"Yes, yes," he said into the telephone. "It's the boss's order. Delivery is for her son Thomas. It's on the second basement level waiting for collection... Yeah, that's right. All for the boy."

The man in the red robe stood silent. Listening.

Her son?

Roland carried on. "Oh and be sure to drop it at the gatehouse with the groundskeeper, not to the kid himself. They'll know what to do...

Could that be his friend on the Minitel screen?

"Don't mess this up, okay?" Roland said, standing from his seat. "If something goes wrong, it's on you. I'm counting on you, understand? This is beyond important."

As he hung up the call, Roland looked up to see the man who was waiting.

"Can I—"

But the room was empty. The man had left.

The large service elevator descended to the sub-levels of the department store. It clacked and whirred as the mechanism sent it down.

Inside, the man dressed as Santa Claus stood motionless, his vacant stare fixed on the glowing floor numbers as they ticked down.

Soon, a loud *ding* echoed as the elevator came to a stop at the second basement level. The sliding doors whined open, letting the staler, cooler air in.

The man leaned forward slightly, peering out of the door down the dim corridors beyond.

It was empty.

The ceiling was low, and the walls were covered with peeling paint and patches of damp. This was part of the store that was not cared for, nor seen by anyone in management.

The only signs of life came from the large room ahead, where a few delivery workers navigated between towers of packages and crates, heads down, busy, and very much unaware of the man in a Santa Clause suit now staring at them from the shadows. Watching for any clues.

A deliveryman walked up to a stack of gift-wrapped boxes, checking against his clipboard.

"This the boss's order?" he called out.

A man in a high-vis vest, the stock manager, gave him a thumbs up. "Yeah, that's it."

"Alright for some, isn't it?" the deliveryman shook his head. "Bet she didn't even pay for these!"

The stock manager chuckled. "Nope. Never does."

From the shadows, the man crept closer, watching as the stack of boxes were placed into the back of an open van. This was all going to his new friend. Thomas. The boy on the Minitel machine who invited him over. The boy who wanted to play a game.

And he would be ready. Ready to play.

He walked forward and ducked down behind a crate, waiting for his moment to move.

"Don't forget the other two!" the stock manager called out, pointing to the remaining load that had not yet been put on the van.

"I got it, I got it..." the deliveryman grumbled.

From behind the pillar, the man looked nervous. He *had* to get that address. He had to find his friend.

In the sitting room, Thomas' combat boots sat neatly in front of the burning fireplace, their laces tucked inside, toes pointing to the now dying embers. Nearby, J.R. walked across the room, his tail swishing, looking for a place to fall asleep.

The lights had been turned down low and the curtains were drawn. Papy and Thomas sat at a table, looking over a sprawling board covered in miniature figures, dice, with piles of worn game cards. A game they had played many times.

Thomas looked at the pieces, his mind clearly elsewhere.

"Are you dreaming, or playing?" Papy asked, tapping the board with a finger. "I'm in the labyrinth, remember? You need to tell me what happens next."

Thomas looked up, pulling himself back to the game. "Oh, sorry," he checked the card in his hand. "You take two hits to the back," he said.

Papy shrugged. "Ah well..."

"Let's see what happens next." Thomas rolled three multi-sided dice across the table. They all settled into a tight spin before landing.

"Nineteen... You've been hit," Thomas said. "So that costs you four points. What do you do?"

Papy leaned forward, with a thoughtful expression. He may not have understood much of this game, but he knew enough. "I'll use my third eye," he announced grandly, "to see who's behind me."

"Okay," Thomas nodded as he picked up a small plastic figure, then placed it on the board. "It's a Troll."

"In that case, I cast a spell of brightness to blind him."

"He shields his eyes," Thomas replied, already rolling again. "What do you do now?"

Papy paused as he looked down at the character sheet next to him. Looking over the wealth of stats which meant little. "I... I don't know."

Thomas noticed his grandfather's confusion, and decided to change the conversation. "You know... Papy... I wanted to ask your opinion on something."

"Oh, yes?" Papy's eyes lit up, happy to avoid the game.

"Sometimes I wonder if Santa Claus *really* exists... And Napoleon, and cavemen and all that... if any of them ever existed. We're told they did. But how do we really know? Just because a book said so? The book could be lying."

The old man looked surprised.

"Let me get this straight. You're not just doubting Santa Claus, you're doubting all human history?"

Thomas shrugged. "Well... there's no proof is there?"

"Oh, there is very much proof," Papy said, sitting back in his chair. "Take cavemen, for example. We've found their drawings. Even their skeletons. Their houses. Their tools."

"But not Santa's," Thomas pointed out. "Nobody's ever found anything about him. No skeleton."

"That's because Santa isn't dead. Obviously... You have to know that just because something cannot be seen, it doesn't mean it doesn't exist. You can't see hope, can you? You can't see love. But they very much exist. Just like this table does." He wrapped his knuckles on the wood, making his point. "You know that space exists, but you have never been up there."

Thomas gave a quiet and uncertain "Yeah," but his brow remained furrowed. "So, what about Vercingetorix?"

"The Gallic chieftain?" Papy said, surprised to hear that name. "How do you know about him?"

"In school, we learned about the Roman wars... They never found his skeleton, did they?"

"No, they did not," Papy admitted.

"Then how do you *know* he was real? If we have no actual proof like a bone."

"Because it's written in history," Papy said with confidence.

"History can lie, though," Thomas replied. "You weren't there. You didn't see him. What if one person made him up, told everyone, and they believed it. Then they told more people."

Papy laughed. "Well, you got me there." But he was not giving in. He thought for a moment. "Tell me, Thomas... do you believe in aliens?"

"Of course," the boy replied, like it was obvious.

"Well, have you seen any?"

Thomas shook his head.

Papy continued. "All we have are people's stories, no actual proof."

Quietly, Thomas replied. "I guess..."

Papy grinned, picking up a small plastic ring from the games board, remembering a move he could make. "Well then, as we have settled that, my next move is to seize the ring!"

Thomas slapped his hand on the table with a laugh. "Bravo! You've done it! You completed the quest. That's a thousand experience points! You can finally level up!"

Papy raised an eyebrow. "What do you mean finally?"

"Listen, Papy. We've been playing this game for two years, and you're still on level one."

The old man smiled and waved the boy over with his hand. "Oh, come here, you little scoundrel. There is something you've forgotten?"

"What is it?" Thomas asked as got up and walked around to his grandfather.

Suddenly, grabbing Thomas, Papy began to mercilessly tickle him.

"You forgot that you are ticklish!" the old man shouted. As Thomas collapsed into laughter, he fell into his grandfather's lap. After a moment, their laughter soon fell away, and they hugged each other.

Thomas kissed his grandfather on the forehead.

"I love you," he said. "But you really have to start getting better at this game."

"My boy," Papy replied. "I would be happy to stay on level one forever, as long as we get to spend time together."

"Yeah." Thomas nodded as he realized something. "Hey, Papy... Could Santa Claus be an alien? That would explain a lot, wouldn't it?"

"Seems like he's been on your mind a lot lately,

hasn't he?" Papy said as he tousled the boy's hair. "Anyway, it doesn't matter. It's bedtime now. We can talk about aliens tomorrow, after he arrives in a spaceship with all your presents... But if you don't go to sleep, he may skip us completely."

Just then, J.R. pricked up his ears and let out a loud bark to the window.

"Hey, you too," Thomas said to his dog. "No barking or you'll get nothing for Christmas, either."

Thomas stood, took his grandfather's hand, and led him out of the room.

As they passed the tree in the lobby, Papy glanced up at it.

"The tree seems to get bigger every year," he mused.

"Well it has to be!" Thomas replied. "What's the point in having a small one?"

Papy laughed as they got to the stairs, the tree lights twinkling behind them.

At the far end of the estate, a Printemps delivery van slowly drove past the open wrought-iron gates. Its engine rumbled as it rolled up the snow-covered driveway to the front of the small gatehouse. Its headlights swung slowly across the window as it came to a stop.

From the driver's side door, the delivery man stepped out, whistling.

Making his way to the back of the van, he jingled his keys.

His whistles soon turned to hum as he unlocked the double doors.

He did not see what was waiting inside.

The doors were pushed open smacking the driver in the face.

Then a blur of red as two arms lunged out from between the boxes and clamped around the delivery driver's throat.

The whistling stopped as the violent grip tightened.

The driver's boots kicked against the van, as the large arms dragged him inside. There was no sound except the gradually wetter thud of a skull hitting against metal. The deliveryman's hands scrabbled uselessly. His veins bulged, as blood poured from his now cracked open head, and the last of the air in his lungs hissed out from between his clenched teeth.

Inside, the man in a Santa Claus suit stood up. Stepping over the driver's twitching, dying body, and jumped down onto the snowy driveway. The front of his suit now sprayed in speckles of blood.

Turning to the gatehouse, the man smiled.

This was indeed the right place, he knew that.

He could feel it. This was the place where his new friend lived.

But he also knew that other people would try stop them from being able to play. They always did when he found a new friend. And he could not let that happen. *Not again.*

The bell rang once, its chime flooding the otherwise quiet living room of the gatehouse.

Charles, the groundskeeper was there, reading a book in the glow of a lamp. Putting it down, he turned to his wife, Linda, who was sipping a cup of tea.

"I'll get it," he said with a smile. "Must be the presents for the boy."

Linda shook her head. "They spoil him too much."

"Not that much," Charles replied.

Opening the door, he could not help but smile at the Santa Claus standing there, his arms full of wrapped boxes.

"Oh, they got you to be dressed up as Santa this year?" Charles said with a chuckle. "Nice touch. Thomas will love that."

Linda walked up behind and noticed the other boxes stacked just beyond the stoop.

"Are *all* of these for Thomas?" she asked.

Charles glanced at her, "Okay, I admit it... You're right, he's spoiled."

Santa didn't say a word. Instead, he raised one gloved finger to his lips. A quiet, playful gesture. But the face behind the fake beard didn't smile. Not even a little.

The room was quiet, save for the ticking of a wall clock by the door.

Thomas was in bed, dressed in his blue pajamas covered in tiny cartoon spaceships printed all over them.

Papy sat on the edge, tucking the covers around him.

At the foot of the bed, J.R. had already made himself comfortable, curled into a warm loaf of fur, with his tail tucked in underneath him.

"Sleep well," Papy said as he kissed Thomas on the cheek.

But Thomas wasn't quite ready.

"Why is Pilou's Mom with him tonight, and mine's not here?" he asked, the question obviously bothering him.

Papy had just begun to stand up from the bed,

but the question stopped him in his tracks. He settled back down.

"Why... because Pilou's Mom doesn't have the same responsibilities as yours, that's why," he said. "Look at all we have, that is because of her, and what she does for us. She said as much this morning. She does all this for us. For you. And anyway, what difference does it make? You'll be asleep soon. She'll be back tomorrow morning, just in time for Santa Claus to have come and gone. And I'm here with you."

"When Dad was here, it wasn't like this," Thomas replied. "Mom always came home. She never spent nights out with that man."

Papy looked at the boy caringly. "Thomas... you've got to stop being so hard on your mom. Tonight, she's working, yes. And if, on other nights, she goes out with... friends. Well, that's normal too. Have you thought about how she might feel?" He hesitated, but continued. "Her not being here doesn't mean she's forgotten about you, or even your father, or that she doesn't love you or him anymore. It just means she needs to see someone other than a grumpy old man and a little genius boy. You can understand that can't you? She deserves more. So much more."

Thomas broke into a small smile. "Little genius?" he said.

"Yes... And look, if you really want her to turn into someone as unbearable as Pilou's mother, then I can guarantee you will soon change your mind and want the space! Imagine her always being there, telling you what to do. She's my daughter and even *I* don't want that!"

Thomas laughed, and he reached out and took his grandfather's hand.

Papy squeezed it gently, and then, he spoke in a hushed voice. "The Sundering Seas between them lay..." he began.

Thomas' voice joined in, finishing the quote: "...and yet, at last, they met once more."

"The Lord of the Rings," Thomas added.

"Could anyone ever truly separate Lúthien from Beren?" he asked.

"No one," Thomas replied.

"Well, then," Papy said, "it's the same with you, your mother and your father. No matter what, you three will always be connected. Even if he is gone or she is not here on some evenings. No one can replace him, and her love for you will never fade."

Thomas nodded.

Papy motioned across the room, to the nylon domed tent that stood by the window. "Let me guess, you're going to go there as soon as I shut the door?"

Thomas smiled, not needing to answer the question.

"Alright, well I won't tell your mother," Papy said, standing at last. "You sleep tight little genius."

"You too grumpy old man."

Papy laughed as he turned to the dog.

"You keep guard okay, J.R.?" he said, also giving him a kiss.

CHAPTER FOUR

The manor was lit by nothing but the December moonlight. There were no lights inside nor out. The only illumination came from the gatehouse. But the light there only showed the horror of what just happened.

Neither Papy nor Thomas heard the pleas for mercy nor the screams that followed coming from Charles and Linda.

From the gatehouse living room, a curtain twitched. A hand slipped beneath it. Pulling the fabric aside just enough for a pair of eyes to peer out.

Behind, the inside was a nightmare. The bodies of the groundskeeper and maid lay sprawled on the floor, their bodies battered and strangled.

As the man in the Santa suit moved away from the window. He carefully stepped over the bruised bodies, and walked through to the kitchenette. There he opened the fridge, and helped himself to a can of beer without asking. The bubbles hissed as he lifted the ring pull.

The rage that was in him had fallen away, and once again he looked calm. Somewhat happy. He looked around as he took a sip of the drink, yet didn't see the horrible massacre he had just committed, but instead a clearer path to seeing his new friend Thomas. He solved a problem, that's all it was.

In Thomas' room, the small domed tent sat opposite the now empty bed. A faint light shone through its nylon as a shadow moved against its inner wall.

The zipper then opened, and Thomas crawled out, careful not to make too much noise. Behind him, J.R. raised his head sleepily.

"Stay here, boy," Thomas whispered, crouching beside his dog. "If I get caught, you can still get *your* presents, okay?"

The dog gave a soft blink, didn't move, and quickly fell back to sleep.

Thomas stood up, ready to put his plan into action.

Walking to the wardrobe in socked feet, he trod as silently as a cat. He slowly opened the door, moved aside the hanging clothes inside, and reached to the back panel. His fingers quickly found the hidden latch. The wood gave way with a soft click, revealing a hidden entrance, leading to a narrow passage beyond.

Thomas was an inventor, a builder, a computer programmer, all at an early age. But he did not need to build these hidden rooms. The manor house was already full of them the day he was born. His father had told him that they used to be servants' access passages, hidden so they wouldn't be seen in the hallways. Thomas always found that idea silly, but now, the passages were solely his domain. His way of getting around the house, all linked to his secret room far below, where his equipment was hidden.

Thomas soon emerged through the shell of the old refrigerator in the basement, brushing dust from his pajamas. Now he wore his armband monitor, whose screen lit up with the black and white camera feed of the lobby.

He walked past the hanging sheets, and through to the staircase that led to the ground floor.

· · ·

The dining room at night was pitch black and quite cavernous. Its high ceilings were covered in shadows and seemed endless, making its walls appear further apart than they actually were. Most children would find this a scary place to be in, but not Thomas. Not even with what once happened here. He had so many cameras set up, so many alarms and traps at the ready, that he felt safe.

He crept into the room silently, barely breathing, stepping toe to heel across the parquet floor. Switching on a lamp as he went by, the room was immediately cast in a calming orange glow.

Getting to the long dining table, he ducked beneath the tablecloth and hid underneath. He settled into position where he could see the fireplace through the gap between the floor and the cloth.

On his armband monitor, he tapped a button. The screen blinked to a different camera feed. It was of his grandfather, asleep in bed, safe and unmoving.

He pressed the button again. The camera view switched once more. This time to the first-floor hallway.

He pressed it again, and the screen showed the dining room. Seen from high above him, perfectly framing the fireplace.

From this vantage point, he could also see his

own foot peeking out from the tablecloth. He quickly retracted it, determined that he had to stay hidden.

He was ready.

The trap for Santa Claus was set.

The clock on the sideboard read 21:50. Not long to go.

Inside the closing department store, the shoppers moved slowly to the exits. Over the intercom, a well-spoken female voice echoed through the aisles.

'This is a message to all Printemps customers, the store will be closing at ten o'clock.' There was a pause, before the voice returned. 'Please proceed to the registers. And from all the staff, we wish you all a very merry Christmas!'

In the offices above the sales floor, Julie dropped a stack of ledgers onto her desk. She looked exhausted after an extremely long and tiring day. The added festive hires outside were a great idea for sales, but it was draining to manage. Something she had found herself doing all day, as no one else was taking any responsibility. She should not have had to have grabbed that girl away from the man in the Santa suit. There should have been managers around, overseeing it all. This, though, would be a problem for another day. All she had to focus on now was getting the last work done so she could go home.

Roland stood at the door to her office, a thin smile, looking as worn out as she was.

"What a day, huh?" he groaned.

Julie slumped in her chair. "And it's not over yet."

"What do you mean it's not over? Stores closed. Everyone has gone home."

She rubbed her tired eyes with her hand. "I still have to go through the receipts. Cash up for the bank."

"Can't that be done Monday?" He sighed.

"And what? Lose two days of interest on ten million francs?" she said. "Not a chance of that. That could be the difference between a good year and a great year."

Roland checked his watch. "Look, Julie, it's ten o'clock on Christmas Eve. No way the bank will do a pick-up now."

"I already called them," she said, flipping open one of the ledgers. "Pickup is at two-thirty am."

Roland groaned overly theatrically, then stomped across the room to take the ledgers from her desk.

"Fine, but *I'll* do it," he said. "*I'm* the only one out of us that has an accounting degree, and no family. So you go home and try to spend Christmas with your son."

He took out his car keys from his pocket and threw them on her desk.

"And take my car, I can get a cab back… If you get out of here now, you'll be up early enough to see Thomas open his presents."

Julie paused, surprised at his generosity. "Are you sure?" she asked. "You don't need me?"

"You're the boss, not a bean counter… And I can handle it, unless you don't trust me?"

She didn't need to answer; she definitely trusted him.

Roland smiled. "Good. I'll set up in the next office, okay? You just go."

As he walked away, Julie's voice followed him.

"Hey, Roland?"

He stopped and glanced back over his shoulder. "Yeah?"

"Thank you. Really. I mean it… And merry Christmas."

He looked at her and smiled as he disappeared through to the next office.

In the bathroom of the gatehouse, the man in the

Santa suit stood in front of a large mirror hung above the porcelain sink.

He stared at himself, at the fake white beard that was strapped over his own brown one. Fastened with threadbare elastic, it didn't look right. It looked fake. Not like the real Santa Claus. Ripping it off, he gazed at his own beard for a few moments, before an idea hit him, and he smiled.

Scurrying out of the room, he reappeared in the bathroom a few moments later, this time holding a can of snow spray.

He shook the can, unable to hide his joy at his idea.

Then he sprayed.

Not the mirror, or the walls. But himself.

Starting with the beard. He lifted the nozzle close, closing his eyes as the aerosol hissed out a thick chemical foam that clung to his facial hair. Then when he had coated his beard, he moved the can to his hair, tilting his head to get the spray on every side.

The fumes from the spray were not pleasant and quite caustic. As he breathed in, the fumes burned his nostrils. But he didn't care. He carried on regardless. Methodically and without any hesitation, coating all the hair that he could.

Soon, his beard was brilliantly white, and his hair looked covered in ice.

By the time the can ran dry, there was no trace of the younger man beneath. He looked, in the failing light, like every child's version of Saint Nicholas, albeit a cheaper version.

As he walked into the living room, over the bodies on the floor, he noticed the clock on the shelf, ticking away the final seconds of the day.

Thirty-five minutes past ten.

He sat in the old rocking chair, and kept his eyes on the time, waiting for midnight.

The dining room was very still. The only sound was the occasional creak of the old house settling, or the groan of an old pipe.

Under the long table, Thomas lay on his stomach, elbows propped on the floor. A torch sat beside him, illuminating a small pile of cards spread out in front. The game he played was simple, childishly so, but he focused all his attention on it, killing time before Santa's arrival. One by one, he laid a card facedown, then slapped the floor beside it, trying to flip it over with the force of the impact. If he did, he moved the card to a winning pile. If not, it went onto the losing pile. It was a silly game, but he kept at it, working through the whole deck, flipping each card with a sharp smack of his palm.

The winning pile greater than its losing counterpart.

A trill from the phone made him jump. He shot up, forgetting the table above him, and hit his head on the wood with a smack.

"Ow!" he cried, recoiling, his hands rubbing his sore head.

He staggered out from under the table, glaring at it as if it were the one to blame for being in his way.

The phone kept ringing loudly.

Thomas rushed over to the sideboard, grabbed the receiver, then scurried back under the table with it, dragging its overly long curly cord with it.

He whispered, "Hello?"

'Hello, Thomas?' Julie said, happy to hear his voice. *'It's Mom, sweetheart. Are you okay?'*

Thomas didn't say anything right away, he just smiled and held the receiver closer.

"I'm good. I was just in bed."

'Really? So you're not staying up to catch Santa?' She let out a small chuckle. *'You know, you shouldn't try to see him. If you do, he gets angry. And then... he turns into an ogre.'*

That made Thomas sit up straighter, eyes wide in the darkness of the table above him. "What?" he said. "An ogre? Is that real?"

'Mmm-hmm,' she said playfully. 'A *big one, too.*
So go back to bed, and believe me, by morning your
presents will have been delivered... Anyway is Papy
there?'

"No he went to bed when I did. He's fast asleep.
I can hear him snoring from my bedroom."

'*Okay, well I'm leaving in a moment. So you*
better have your eyes closed too by the time I get
home, or I might turn into an ogre as well!'

"Okay," Thomas said quickly, squeezing his eyes
shut. "My eyes are closed."

'*You have to be in bed as well!'*

"Fine, I'll go up now..."

Thomas was picturing Santa turning into an
Ogre. He had never heard of that before, but to him,
this new information made sense. It explained why
no one had ever caught the man on camera.

'*I'm sending you a big kiss, right on the cheek.*
Now hurry to bed, okay?'

"Shhh!" Thomas whispered. "I'm asleep already,
you don't wanna wake me up do you? Now hurry
back here... Love you."

Julie's hands remained cradling the receiver for a
moment before she set it back in place.

She didn't get up right away. Instead, she sat at her desk, thinking of how lucky she was. Despite the tragedy in their family, where most families would fall apart, theirs grew stronger. Papy and Thomas were everything to her.

The clock in the dining room struck midnight with twelve chimes, that rang through the house.

Under the dining room table, Thomas sat up, shocked at the sound.

He had fallen asleep. He hadn't meant to, and now, waking, he grimaced in annoyance. He was just about to poke his head out to check the clock when he heard something.

Something that he didn't recognise. Something coming from the fireplace. A scraping sound.

He turned, and peeked through the gap between the tablecloth and the floor.

Above the burned-out coal from the last lit fire, something was dangling down.

A rope.

It hung down the chimney shaft, swaying slightly above the embers.

Thomas couldn't breathe as he peered out in awe.

It was finally happening, he thought.

There was that sound again.

Scraping.

And then he saw it.

Red fabric, lined with thick white fur, descended slowly above the hearth, hanging above two large dirty boots, that crunched against the stone, as they held grip.

His gaze didn't move from the fireplace, but he also remembered his mother's words. That Santa would turn into an ogre if he was seen. Remembering this, Thomas backed away slowly, hiding deeper in the shadows of the table's underside.

He should have pressed the camera record button on his armband monitor. That was the plan. Catch it all on tape. Capture Santa Claus digitally for the world to marvel at. But Thomas' hands couldn't move. He sat still, not only nervous but overwhelmed. Not only the unfolding impossibility that he'd dared to believe in now finally coming true, but also that he might be in danger by an angry mystical man.

Ogres had bad tempers after all. That's what the books said.

He wished he had realized earlier, but he had

forgotten to shut his bedroom door before he left through the hidden passageway. And from that room, sensing the intruder from upstairs, J.R. bounded into the dining room.

Yet he was not the happy, loving dog he usually was. Not with this man coming down the chimney. The dog ran in at full speed, growling loudly, with teeth bared to the gums.

Thomas panicked, throwing both arms forward.

No! No, stop!

But he didn't say those words aloud, he only mouthed them, afraid of making a sound. Afraid of the ogre's wraith.

J.R. growled louder as he launched at the man in red.

Thomas couldn't see much.

He could not see the man react brutally. One swift movement as his hand reached for the table, gripped a cake-serving knife, turned, and brought it down with terrible force on the dog simply trying to protect his house.

There was no bark.

No whine.

Nothing except the thud of J.R.'s lifeless body slumping to the floor.

The serving knife stuck through his skull.

He had no time to feel pain or understand what had happened. He was dead before his body collided with the parquet.

Thomas couldn't scream. His mouth was open wide, but no sound came out. His body was locked in place, as a panic crawled up his spine. Tears fell down his cheeks in quiet streams.

The man in red turned to walk out of the room, but his boot caught on something—a cable that stretched across the floor. A curly wire trailing from the telephone on the sideboard, to the receiver that was now beside Thomas. The one he had forgotten to put back.

The man could not see what was under the table, behind the tablecloth, but he had a feeling of what was there. Of *who* was there.

"Thomas?" he said. His voice was full of expectant glee. "Is that you under there?"

That was all Thomas needed to hear to force him to run.

From the other end of the table, he shot out, sprinting out of the room, heading to the stairs.

"Papy! Papy!" he shouted at the top of his lungs, taking two steps at a time. "The ogre's here! *The ogre's here!*"

Behind him, from the dining room, came a laugh.

Not a cruel one, but a laugh full of amusement. The man dressed as Santa Claus was delighted that his new friend, Thomas, wanted to play. This was a game of chase. A game the man was more than happy to join in with.

"I'll give you to the count of twenty!" he called out.

Thomas ran into Papy's bedroom at full speed, slamming the door behind him.

His grandfather was already half awake, having heard Thomas' cries. His eyes struggling to open as his grandson stood at the end of his bed.

"Papy," Thomas shouted again, tears pouring as he tried to catch his breath.

"What's going on, Tommy?" the old man asked, worriedly sitting up. "Why are you crying?"

Grabbing a wooden chair, Thomas dragged it across the room. He hurriedly wedged the back of it under the door handle. Then leaned his weight into it. Trying as hard as he could to stop anyone from being able to come in.

He could barely catch his breath, as he spoke between emotional gasps. "It's Santa... He's an ogre... Just like Mom said... He... He killed J.R."

"*What?*" His grandfather stared,

uncomprehending. "An ogre killed... What are you talking about?" *Was this some kind of terrible prank?* the old man could not help but think.

Thomas didn't answer, he just ran over to the telephone on the bedside table.

But when he lifted the receiver, there was no dial tone, just another voice on the other end. A voice that spoke from another phone in the house.

"Hello, Thomas," the man said. "Are you enjoying our game so far?"

Thomas immediately dropped the receiver.

He then grabbed his grandfather's hand and pulled him out of the bed.

In the lobby beneath the stairs, the man stood gripping the phone. With a grunt, he tore it from the telephone base. The cord snapped away with a spark. He discarded the broken handset onto the floor, where it clattered and bounced across the marble before coming to a stop.

This, though, wasn't enough. There was more than one phone in the building, and he didn't have time to find them all.

He turned, and that's when he saw it. A small utility cupboard tucked along the wall.

Still holding the cake-serving knife in his hand,

its blade still wet with J.R.'s blood, he grinned. Pulling the cupboard open, it was just as he thought —there sat the main wires for the house. Specifically one box that stated *France Télécom* on its casing. Grabbing the wires running out of them, he raised his knife. One clean slice, and it was over. He cut straight through them, the wires splitting easily under the blade with a rubbery snap. Severing the house's connection to the outside world.

Another chuckle came from his throat. He was winning already, he thought.

The window opened with a crack as the ice snapped away from its frame. Thomas helped his still-confused grandfather over the sill and out onto the balcony. Without shoes or coat, the old man moved slowly, his hands gripping the stone balustrade for balance. He did not know what had gotten into Thomas, but he could tell one thing. The boy was genuinely scared. And after what had happened to his father, he knew, for everyone's sake, he had to play along until he could figure out what was happening.

They crossed the length of the building in silence, save for the ragged whimpers Thomas could not help but make. The image of J.R. falling dead to the floor was hitting him hard, dragging along with them the memories of his father, also lying dead on the same dining room floor.

The door to Papy's bedroom gave way on the fifth kick, splintering inward under the man's full weight. He stomped hard at the frame, and when the door finally cracked in two, sending the chair that was braced against it, flying across the room, he stood breathing with a maniacal grin and peered inside. Looking for the boy, but no one could be seen.

From somewhere else in the house came the sound of glass shattering. A sound he heard.

He turned toward it, with a surprised expression.

Thomas' bedroom window had a large hole at the bottom of the pane, smashed by his elbow. He reached in from outside, unlatched the window, and pulled it open.

He quickly ushered his grandfather inside.

"Hurry," the boy said in a scared whisper.

Landing on the carpet, Thomas rushed across the room, opened his wardrobe doors, and pushed his grandfather inside. The old man struggled to keep up. His chest was hurting from the exertion, and he was still so lost, not understanding what was happening.

"Why are we hiding in here?"

Thomas closed the door behind them. "Please, just trust me," he said.

From the inside, Thomas pushed aside his hanging clothes and opened the hidden panel on the back wall.

As it opened, the darkness inside waited for them, and Papy looked aghast.

Following his grandfather, Thomas slipped into the narrow passageway, moving the clothes back and shutting the hatch behind him.

The wooden stairs creaked beneath their weight as they walked down into Thomas' secret room. As he hit the light switch, the bulbs sprung to life, illuminating the large hidden space.

Papy glanced around at the shelves of toys, electronics, even a play-size Spitfire that hung from the ceiling on wires. There were tin soldiers, stuffed animals, puzzle boxes, model trains, mechanical horses. It felt less like a playroom than a storage unit. He thought he had seen it all, but when he saw the rope bridge that stretched across the room, from one side to the other, he could not help but speak up.

"What is all this, Thomas?" he asked.

Thomas crossed the rope bridge first, turning every few steps to make sure Papy was behind him.

"Come on," he said, pointing to the far end of the room. "We've to get to Mom's car. This is the only way out."

"What about the keys?"

"I left them in the ignition... Come on."

On the first floor, the man in the Santa suit made his way down the corridor, the bloody cake-serving knife still in his grasp. He looked calm, and his smile had not left his face.

He wasn't hurrying.

There was no need.

He was enjoying the game far too much.

The door to the old refrigerator swung open in the basement of the house. Thomas stepped out first. He turned back, offering a hand, and helped his grandfather out, who groaned from the exertion. Papy stumbled as he clambered out, but regained his footing with one hand against the wall. He could not play along any longer. He hurt all over.

"Please Thomas, you *have* to tell me what's happening, right now. No more games, okay?"

"Hurry," Thomas urged.

The laundry room stretched ahead of them, lit only by the single bulb that shone above the drying sheets. Now, they looked ghostly, as their thin cotton flittered in the light breeze that came down from the rest of the house.

Thomas hurried on, weaving between the linens, holding Papy's hand tightly, guiding him through the gaps of washing.

As they got to the garage, the air had become freezing.

The Ford Taunus waited for them.

Tools were scattered across the floor where Thomas had last worked on the car.

He had been disappointed when his mother said she would not be driving this to work, but here and now, he was relieved she had gotten a taxi.

He opened the driver's door as Papy moved to the other side, slower than the boy wanted.

"Come on!" Thomas said. "Hurry, get in!"

As Thomas got behind the wheel, he reached across to the glove compartment. The plastic remote control he pulled out had only button. One that he quickly pressed.

The button made a clicking sound, and the

heavy garage door began to rise, clacking loudly as it rolled upward.

Thomas turned the key in the car's ignition.

But there was nothing. The engine didn't start.

He tried again.

The engine clicked, but refused to turn over.

Upstairs, in the boy's bedroom, the window still hung open where they had climbed inside from the balcony.

The man in the Santa suit leaned out over the sill, into the night air and listened.

He soon heard the garage door opening.

Thomas gritted his teeth. Turning the ignition over again.

"Come on, come on," he said in a panic. "Start. Please start!"

His foot jammed down hard on the pedal, as the engine growled, before giving a choking splutter, and cutting off again.

"I fixed you!" Thomas said, "You can't be broken. I—"

He didn't finish his sentence. His attention was

drawn to the windscreen as Papy let out a shocked gasp.

Standing there, in the headlight's glow just outside the garage, was Santa Claus.

He remained motionless in the centre of the beam, staring back at Thomas through the glass.

Papy's mouth hung open in shock as his hands clutched his knees. He didn't say a word, but his thoughts were in a daze. He remembered what Thomas had told him. That Santa was an ogre, and he killed J.R. He did not know how much was true or false, but he could not deny the man standing now before them.

Thomas turned the key again, and as if by some divine intervention, the engine turned and caught.

The boy didn't spare a second. His foot slammed on the accelerator pedal.

But the man dressed as Santa didn't flinch. He remained exactly where he was, blocking the way out. Not afraid of a car.

Thomas looked at the man, then at his grandfather, then back again.

"What do I do?" he asked, voice rising. "Papy, *what do I do?*"

The old man didn't falter. "You run him over, now!"

"I can't! He's... he's not moving!"

The car then shook as it stalled, the engine cutting out.

"No, no, no," Thomas pleaded as he turned the key one more time, but now, the engine didn't answer. No lights. No clicks. Nothing. The battery was totally drained. The car would not start now, no matter what the boy tried.

The headlights had also flicked out, and the man in front of them was shrouded in shadow, now just a black silhouette against the moonlight.

He then began walking forward, into the garage, toward the car.

Thomas scrambled to roll up his open window by hand.

"Close it, Papy.... your side... *close* it!"

The old man fumbled for the handle and wound it as fast as he could. The glass inched upward, as the handle kept sticking.

Thomas then locked the driver's door. Papy did the same on his side. The locks clicked with a sound far too quiet to allow them to feel any safer.

Outside, Santa reached the hood of the car.

He leaned across it, until his deep breaths were close enough to fog the windscreen. Then, without any warning, he threw his head back and slammed it brutally into the glass. Head butting the glass, and fracturing it on impact. The cracks shot out like a web, crawling out across the pane in jagged lines.

The man, unfazed, stared in at Thomas through the cracks, as the new wound on his forehead started to bleed down his face.

He then stood up and started to circle around the back of the car, vanishing from view.

Then the first blow came.

Metal buckled inward on the left side of the car, as a blunt object, something very heavy, slammed into it.

Thomas managed to get a glimpse in the rearview mirror. The man was holding a sledgehammer.

He raised the weapon, and it soon came crashing down into the taillight, breaking it on impact. Before waiting, the man turned and did the same to the other side. Glass sprayed out across the garage as the hammer demolished them.

Inside, Thomas flinched and reached out to grab hold of his grandfather's hand. But Thomas wasn't the only one scared. His grandfather was just as petrified as he was.

In the mirror, Thomas saw the man start to walk back around the front of the car. The same blank expression on his face yet leaking an immense joy.

Thomas spoke quietly, forcing himself to keep as calm as possible.

"Listen to me, Papy. When I count to three, open your door as hard as you can. Slam it into the wall, okay? If you do that hard enough, the door will stick there. Then we can run back into the house. Got it?"

"Got it," Papy nodded. "I think."

The man was raising the hammer once more.

It came down with a deafening noise at the front of the car, where the bumper cracked off and fell to the floor.

"One," Thomas said.

They each slowly unlocked their doors.

The man ahead bent down.

"Two."

The man stood up, the bumper now in his hands.

"Three."

Both Thomas and Papy threw their weight into the doors. They flung open, hitting the garage walls on either side, metal screeched against concrete as they jammed in place, wedging solidly.

The man grunted as he hurled the bumper into the already fractured windshield, now shattering it completely, as it broke through.

Glass sprayed everywhere, but Thomas and Papy were already out of their seats.

They scrambled out and ran to the rear of the

car, not looking back once. Thomas' hand met with his grandfather's sleeve, pulling him along as they fled back through the house, toward the secret passageway they'd come through.

Behind them, Santa snarled angrily. He was now losing the game, and didn't like that one bit. He strode around to one of the wedged car doors and tried to ram it with his arm, but it didn't move. He kicked it as hard as he could, but it still blocked his way.

Giving up, he climbed onto the hood of the Ford and stomped over its chassis, crumpling the roof in under his weight as he went.

This small delay was enough time for Thomas.

He and his grandfather had run down the steps into the basement, crossed into the side room, and threw open the fake refrigerator door, soon vanishing inside to his secret room.

Seconds later, the man dressed as Santa Claus came in. He walked through the laundry room, the sheets still waving from being pushed aside moments before.

His forehead was wet: blood from the wound on his forehead mixing with sweat, trickling down into his white-painted beard. He grabbed one of the drying sheets, wiped his face, and walked on.

When he got to the side room, the man expected to see the boy and the old man crouching in a corner, trying to hide from him. Then, when he would walk in, they would have lost the game. He would have won, and then the next game could start.

But now, he stood in the middle of the small room, panting, wondering where they went.

He was so sure that they had to have come this way.

CHAPTER FIVE

Papy and Thomas emerged from the passageway, and into the manor's secret room.

The old man spoke quietly, thinking that whoever that intruder was might still hear him. "How did that man get in? You said he was in the dining room when you saw him, right?"

Thomas walked ahead, not looking back. "He came down the chimney," he said.

Papy frowned. "But what about the alarm? Why didn't it go off?"

Thomas turned with a look of guilt on his face. "Because I shut it off," he said. "I had to. How else was Santa supposed to come in without waking anyone up? I just wanted to see him... That's all... But..."

Papy looked confused, trying to figure it all out.

He then motioned around the room. "Okay then, what about this room then?" he said. "Where are we? How come I've never been in here before?"

"It's my secret room," Thomas replied. "No one knows it's here. Not even Mom. It was just between me and Dad... He told me to keep it secret. And now I'm letting you in on it."

"And all these toys?"

"They're his. And his dad's. And there's my toys too. All the ones Mom gets me go in here."

"I did wonder where they all went. You never have that many in your room," Papy shook his head. "I thought you threw them away or broke them."

Feeling the ache all over his body, he then hobbled across to a wicker chair and slumped into it. "This is all just... so confusing. The man... This room... It feels like a dream... or a nightmare... I'm not sure which."

Somewhere above them, faint and muffled, a telephone began to ring.

Papy lifted his head slightly, listening. "That must be the phone in the attic... In your mother's office. It's working?"

"I'll go see," Thomas said.

"*No*," Papy immediately replied. "You stay here. I'll go. Not with that man out there."

"You can't even see properly."

"I see just fine."

"No, you don't. Stop pretending."

Papy couldn't really argue. Thomas was right. His eyesight was so bad, he probably would not even make it to Julie's office, let alone find the phone in there.

Thomas stepped closer and knelt beside his chair. "Papy, we can't just stay here and wait for Mom to get back. We have to warn her, and tell the police."

"But it's too dangerous for you."

"It's dangerous for her too." Thomas snapped.

"Please, Thomas... Tell me. And no fairytales this time. Do you know who that man is?"

Thomas cocked his head. "Who is he? I told you who he is. He's Santa. He came down the chimney. But then I saw him. And just like Mom told me, he turned into an ogre... because he doesn't like being seen... And..." He suddenly remembered J.R. and felt his stomach drop. He gritted his teeth to push the memory away.

"Thomas..." Papy said, feeling like he knew less than he did a moment ago. "We *need* to stay safe."

"I am... I have all the cameras, remember," he motioned to his armband monitor, tapping on the buttons, and cycling through the camera's feeds.

Showing them to Papy. "You want to know where he is right now?"

He flicked through a few more shots until the staircase came into view. The man walked past it.

"He's right there... I can see him. So I'll take another way. I know this place better than he does... And besides, I'm really quiet."

His eyes widened as a thought struck him. He jumped up and rushed back to his bank of computer equipment. "I just remembered, we can use these," he called back, rummaging through one of the low drawers.

"Ah ha!" he exclaimed, pulling out a walkie-talkie. He quickly checked the batteries before hurrying back and handing one to his grandfather.

"Take this. We'll stay in touch the whole time."

Meanwhile, the phone upstairs kept ringing.

Papy looked at the walkie, then at Thomas. "If I said no, you're going to go anyway, aren't you?"

Thomas smiled. "Ten-Four, good buddy."

The Porsche cut through the falling snow at speed along the narrow road. On either side, the leafless branches of the trees bent under the force of strong winds the storm had brought.

Julie held the wheel, trying to focus on the road

as the windscreen wipers worked their hardest to clear her vision.

Her eyes flicked to the dashboard clock, then back to the road.

She had called the house over a dozen times now. The main phone line was dead, and her office line just rang. It didn't matter that it was the middle of the night. It never did. She knew Thomas would be awake, or at least wake when he heard the phone. Most nights when she came home late, Thomas would be awake, or wake up as soon as the door slammed. He never slept well. Which is why this was so strange that no one answered.

She reached for the car phone once more, tapped the redial button, and waited for the ring.

It did.

Continuously.

Until it cut off.

The man in the Santa suit was still moving. Room by room by room. He walked into each one, checking the corners, the doors, the cupboards... in any place a person may hide. He moved slowly and methodically. This was a great game, he thought. One he was determined to win.

He didn't call out, or make much of a sound. He didn't want to give his new friend an advantage.

Thomas, now out of pajamas and dressed in his commando gear, crept through the first-floor hallway as he had many times before. His face was painted with streaks of polish, and his red bandana wrapped around his forehead. He moved low and slow, checking the video feed on his wrist every few steps, flipping through the cameras in quick succession, making sure he knew where Santa Claus was at all times. This wasn't playtime. This was tracking for real.

On the screen he saw the family's games room. And standing in the middle was the man, looking around.

Thomas turned sharply down another corridor. He needed to go down a level to avoid crossing the man's paths, to get to the east wing, and to his mother's office in that attic. To where her working phone was.

In the games room, the man had stopped.

He had heard something... Not anything loud, but *something*.

A soft whirring.

He looked around. Everything was still.

But he could still hear it. Barely.

As his eyes drifted along the curtains, he caught a small light coming from the wall above it. A small orange dot. The sound was coming from there.

He stepped closer.

And there it was. A tiny security camera whirring away.

He stared at it and could not help but smile.

"Bravo," he said, under his breath.

On the staircase, running down to the ground floor, Thomas moved fast, too fast. Too panicked.

As his foot hit the marble, his toe caught on something he hadn't noticed. The broken phone receiver lying on the floor. Kicking it, it sent the receiver noisily clattering across the lobby.

Scared, Thomas ran back and pressed himself up against the wall, hiding in case that noise alerted the ogre.

Ducking behind the suit of armor, he quickly checked the camera feed on his armband.

Almost on cue, he watched as the man lifted a chair up and hurled it up at the camera. Up at him.

Thomas jumped as the camera feed broke and

went to static. The colliding chair ending its surveillance.

"Please no," he said.

Forcing himself to move, Thomas ran down a hallway as he checked the feeds on his armband. One shot after another became white noise, as the man rushed from room to room, finding and breaking every camera he could find.

The man entered the music room. He kept his gaze upward, staring for the orange dot, for the camera. He now knew how the boy was able to hide so well without being caught.

Thomas slipped into the living room, keeping low and against the wall.

He kept pausing to cycle through the feeds, but few worked. Static. Static. Static. Empty room. Static. Empty room. Static.

But even through the feeds still working, the man was nowhere to be seen.

Upstairs in the library, the last working camera on that level went dark.

. . .

Thomas kept his eye on the screens, finding any working camera, but he had no idea where the man went. He stepped forward, back into the hallway.

He quickly got to the staircase and rushed upward, needing to get to the attic as quickly as possible. To get to the phone.

When Thomas got to the first-floor landing, ready to run through the gallery wing, he turned the corner into a hallway, and came to a shocked stop.

There he was.

The man with the bright yellow scarf, dressed as Santa Claus. The man who killed J.R. The ogre.

Standing with a smile on his face at the other end of the hall.

Their eyes met.

There was at least ten metres between them.

The man stood watching.

Thomas could hardly breathe. He had to focus. He had to think. He then realized where the man was standing.

Fingers trembling, he punched in a code on his wristband.

A mechanical groan rolled through the walls, as the security shutters of the house began to close over. The metal panels slammed down over every door and window on all floors one at a time. And as they did, the locks snapped into place. *Clang, clang, clang.*

Every exit was quickly sealed.

Thomas was too nervous. He had typed the wrong code.

The man moved slowly forward, ready to end the game.

Thomas tried again. Punching the intended code slower.

This time, it worked.

The rug gave way, as the trap door underneath the man opened with a heavy slam.

As it did, the man fell with a terrified look of shock.

He was safe, though, as the net had caught him, pulling tight as he landed five feet down.

Thomas raced down the hallway to the gallery corridors. Jumping over the newly opened trap and carried on without looking.

The corridors that held the old oil paintings in the east wing of the manor were labyrinthine, as they snaked their way along. There were no rooms off any of this space, just more art-lined corridors, as it was all its own art space. This gallery was not something of his parents' making. But was from his father's parents who collected Baroque art.

This was not part of the house that Thomas liked to be in. It was too much of a maze that made him feel claustrophobic, not to mention the dark and scary paintings.

The faces glared at him out as he passed. Men in powdered wigs. Angels in velvet dresses. Battles, mythological and real. All kinds of subjects from the same era. As he raced by corner after corner, he eventually came to a dead end.

Damn, he thought, as he realized he ran the wrong way.

He backed up, tried again and took off down the corridor once more.

But every corner looked the same. The paintings looked the same. The same dark look that was no fun to look at.

He came to a standstill as the same dead end came up on him again. He had run in a circle.

He needed to think.

Turning, he saw it: a narrow corridor to his left. One he had not been down. Easy to miss in this sprawling wing.

He darted down it.

· · ·

Back in the hallway trap, the man tore at the net with both hands. It resisted at first, then gave in as his strength ripped their fibres apart. He soon pulled himself free and got to his feet.

Thomas didn't hear the man laughing and clapping his hands behind him as he climbed out of the trap. Thomas had no idea how much this man was enjoying tonight. He was too busy running.

The narrow corridor twisted ahead, leading exactly where he needed to go, to the staircase to the east wing attic. The steps rose steeply in front of him, and from above the phone's ringing soon cut off once more.

He couldn't wait. He ran up as fast as he could. He had to call his mother. The police. Anyone.

The attic office was dark and empty. Only moonlight through the windows provided any light.

The hatch in the floor opened as Thomas walked up and ran to the desk.

He reached out for the receiver... but someone else grabbed it first.

"Do you want me to dial for you, Thomas?" the

grinning face of Santa Claus said. This ogre leaned out of the shadows, holding the revolver in his hands.

Thomas recoiled, wanting to scream. How long had he been lost in the gallery? So long that the man had time to run in front of him and find his way.

The man threw the phone on the desk and hurried as Thomas went to run back.

He was faster than the boy, and made it to the staircase first. Blocking any escape, the man lifted his foot and kicked the attic hatch shut.

Thomas could not hold his scream in as he ran over to the far side of the attic, as far away from the ogre as he could. His screams quickly turned to sobs as he got to the round window.

"Where can you go?" the man said with a smile. "I have won already."

Thomas knew of only one way he could go, as he flipped the window's latch.

As the pane opened, the snow outside had turned into a blizzard. The flakes hit him instantly as the wind billowed inside.

Thomas was terrified, and unable to think straight as he climbed out onto the roof.

Up there, from this window there was no wide balcony. No balustrade. Just the angled pitch of the tiles below his feet.

He sobbed as he pressed close to the slate and, one step at a time, made his escape.

Leaning out after him, the man looked impressed.

"Thomas?" he called out. "Make sure you don't fall. It's dangerous up here." He spoke not out of sarcasm, but genuine concern.

But Thomas didn't look back. He didn't look down. His eyes were fixed on the top of the roof, on the place where the slope rose toward the other wing of the house.

His vision was blurred with tears as his head began to hurt.

He may have loved playing war games. He may have protected this house with traps and cameras, but now he wanted it all to stop. He wanted J.R. back. He wanted his mother home. He wanted his father...

More tears followed.

"Daddy," he cried. "Mommy... Please..."

But despite his upset, he kept on going.

Behind, the attic window had been pulled shut. Cutting off any chance of retreat.

Above, the snow came down so hard it almost looked like he was in a snow globe, crawling along the top of the house, getting swallowed by the white downpour.

Julie drove with one hand on the wheel, the other pressing the car's phone hard against her ear.

"Roland, I've been calling my house, the line's dead."

'*Did you try the private line?*' his voice asked, coming through the speakers.

"Of course I did. That works fine, but no one's picked up. It rang for a while... Now it's just busy."

'*Well, they're probably asleep. It's really late you know?*"

Beneath the lights of the department store office, Roland sat surrounded by towers of receipts and invoices on his desk. He was exhausted, stifling a yawn as he spoke on the phone.

"Alright, don't panic. I've no idea why it's busy. But it's nearly two am!... How about you call your staff and get them to check the house? I'll keep trying your house. That sound good?"

'*Okay*, fine,' came Julie's reply.

"Good... Talk soon."

He hung up and was already dialing again. But just as Julie had said, the main line was dead. Without hesitation, he redialed her office number, both numbers memorized. He was certain Julie didn't know he knew them off by heart. Just as he was equally sure she had no idea what his telephone number was. Or even his middle name.

When the office line finally connected, there was nothing but the shrill tone of a busy line.

He hung up and dialed again.

It was still busy.

And again.

Still busy.

He kept on trying. Over and over.

Anything for Julie.

In the empty attic office of the manor house, the telephone was off the hook, abandoned as it hung to the floor. The round window shut firmly, keeping the storm and Thomas out.

In the car, Julie was now dialing the gatehouse.

She felt some relief knowing that Charles the gatekeeper and Linda the maid were always in, and should be able to sort all this out. She felt quite stupid for not thinking of trying them before Roland had suggested it.

But there was no relief as she had hoped for. The

line just rang and rang. No answer machine. Just a ringing tone.

Far above her concern, beyond the reach of a phone call, Thomas was still climbing along the roof. The snow was now relentless and came down like a sheet.

The slate tiles were slippery with the snowfall, as he moved across slowly. Carefully. Despite the tears that still fell. Despite the heartache he felt. He pushed himself on.

A chimney stack was now a few feet away, and after an unsteady few steps, he reached it, immediately hugging onto its brickwork for dear life.

Maybe he could climb into the house like Santa had done? Looking around, he wiped his wet eyes, focussing to make sure there were no other guests up here. Ones that had pulled a sled. If Santa turned into an ogre when someone saw him, what would Donner, Dancer, Dasher, Prancer, Vixen, Blitzen, Comet, Cupid and Rudolph become? Werewolves?

He grabbed either side of the chimney and tried to scale it, but as he did, a tile broke loose beneath his foot, causing him to lose his balance, and he slipped.

It was a breathless and panicked moment where

gravity nearly took him down to his demise. But he managed to catch himself... just. His arms reached out and gripped the brick. He held his weight for dear life. His muscles strained and trembled, as his breath puffed out.

When he finally pulled himself behind the chimney, so that the brick blocked the slope of the roof, his body fell against it.

He shivered as he curled into a ball. Not knowing what to do.

Then a noise cut through the dark snowstorm.

A sound Thomas felt a sudden pang of hope for.

The faint sound of a phone ringing.

But not one from in the house. Instead, it came from somewhere across the grass. His eyes moved to the gatehouse. Through the storm, he could see their window was lit, but he could not see a silhouette beyond the curtains.

The ringing continued for a few moments, before stopping, then starting again.

No one was answering the call, but someone was insistent to connect.

Thomas was freezing, upset and bereft as he sat behind the chimney, listening to the faint phone.

With numb fingers, he unhooked the walkie-talkie from his belt, extended its antenna, and pressed the talk button. He didn't want to use this.

Papy was not able to do much to help. He was a frail old man... but Thomas needed to hear a loving voice.

"Thomas calling Papy," he whispered. "Papy, come in..."

Static sounded in reply.

He tried again. More urgently, trying to disguise any upset in his tone.

"Thomas calling Papy. Are you there? Papy, please... answer me!"

He didn't. Not for another four calls.

In the secret room, deep in the manor's belly, the walkie-talkie crackled.

Papy fumbled with the plastic device, the call coming through having woken him up. He didn't want to fall asleep, especially when Thomas was in so much danger, but his age, his condition, it was beyond his control.

"Hello? Thomas is that you?" he said into the walkie-talkie. "Sorry, I... I couldn't find the button. You know how it is..." He trailed off, feeling the shame that he was there the moment the call came through. "Are you okay? Please tell me it's over?"

. . .

On the roof, Thomas gave a small smile that hardly even cracked his cheeks.

"Yeah... yeah, I'm fine," he said, lying through his chattering teeth. "The ogre got to the phone. But don't worry, Papy... I've been thinking. I need to get to my bedroom. I can send messages out on my computer. Someone'll definitely pick them up... You don't have to worry. I've got everything under control. Okay?"

He didn't have anything under control. Sure, that was a viable plan, but he had no idea how to do it. Not without the use of his cameras.

'Please call me often, okay?' Papy said. 'And most of all, be careful. You have to be careful. If you see a chance to get out, do it."

After they said goodbye, Thomas retracted the walkie's antenna, and clipped it back onto his belt.

"Stop crying solider," he whispered, as he steeled himself and looked around. Just ahead was the highest stretch still to climb, the peaked roof of the main house. On that part of his home was another window. A window he never locked.

With just one more push, he could do it.

"If Rambo could do this... So can I."

He nodded to himself, then moved up the slope of tiles.

CHAPTER SIX

Inside the manor, a small window eased inward, pushed from the outside. Thomas, trembling and cold, fell inside, collapsing onto the carpeted floor. He was in his bedroom. His skin felt numb, and his limbs stiff. The journey from the chimney to here may have been short, but it was quite treacherous and below freezing.

The lights were off, and the glow of his Minitel computer screen spilled across the carpet. He quickly checked his armband monitor, at the few camera feeds that remained active, but he could not see the ogre in any of the shots.

He dragged himself to his feet and over to his desk, sitting down on his chair. He pulled the keyboard closer, ready to type.

. . .

At the department store, the printer in the office sprang to life. Loudly unspooling paper as the printer ribbon zipped back and forth, inking the paper. This was a printer directly connected to the Minitel computer.

From his desk in one of the adjacent rooms, Roland didn't notice the noise. Since they set up the Minitel computer for employee communications, it had remained inactive. It was an idea he had as head of human resources. But no one ever used it. This might have been the first time the printer function actually worked. So much for a brave new world of technology.

He was too busy redialing Julie's office phone at the manor house to hear the *kachunk chk-chk-chk-chk* of the printer.

Pilou stirred in his sleep.

His small bedroom was lit by a nightlight, not that he would admit his fear of the dark to anyone.

Breaking the silence, his Minitel computer sprang to life with a loud chime. Almost immediately Pilou woke up to the noise. He sat up in his bed, confused and yawning.

The screen flashed at him with a *'new message'* notification. Immediately he knew who it was.

Thomas had customized his Minitel to allow them to communicate with each other this way, and it was only Thomas who had his contact details.

He padded out of his bed and over to the desk.

Despite his bleary eyes and the low light in the room, he could read the message on the screen clearly. His expression changed as his tiredness all but melted away, leaving a horrible sinking feeling of dread in its place.

Papy couldn't sit still anymore. His whole body felt sore. Every bone, muscle, and tendon ached. Something he never got used to at his age. Yes, he was old, but he still felt young in his mind. His body, though, never got that message, as day by day he felt the years increasingly taking their toll. Soreness and pain came from even simple things like sitting down too long. He unsteadily stood to stretch his legs.

Looking around the secret room, he was still astonished that it even existed. How could anyone hide a room this size? The manor was large, but not so large that a ballroom-sized space could remain hidden.

Everywhere he looked was packed with teddy bears, action figures, board games, and toys of every kind. It didn't just look like a second-hand department store, it *felt* like one, cluttered and chaotic.

As he took the first step, his foot caught on a toy robot lying on the floor, and he lost his balance. Stumbling forward, he managed to grip himself on one of the tall, freestanding shelves, narrowly stopping himself from falling. But as he did, his weight caused the whole shelving unit to wobble, then give into gravity as it toppled over. The unit crashed loudly to the ground.

In the laundry room, the sound of the falling shelves hitting the floor echoed faintly through its brick walls.

Someone heard it.

The man in the Santa suit paused mid-step. He had come down to the basement again, sure he had missed something from the last time. Knowing his new friend had to have been hidden down here before.

He followed the reverberating sound into the side room. And walked over to one of the only things stood here: the old refrigerator at the far wall.

Confused, he reached for the handle and yanked it open. Not knowing what to expect, he certainly did not think he would find an absence. No shelves.

No food. Just a gaping hole. A black emptiness cut through the fridge and into the crawlspace beyond.

Papy looked at the fallen shelves and all the toys that had been cast to the floor. His eyesight was barely able to focus, the wreckage in front of him was merely a wash of colour. But he wanted to try and tidy this up.

Bending over painfully, he quickly stood again as the sound of heavy footsteps, dragged his attention. Footsteps from the direction of the entrance.

He turned, listening, with a look of worry, as he squinted to the other side of the room.

"...Tommy?" he whispered, cautiously.

Quickly, he took out the walkie-talkie from his pajama pocket and pressed the button. "Thomas?" he said into it. "Is that you? Are you here?"

Back in his bedroom, Thomas was still typing on the keyboard. Sending message after message to every Minitel contact he could think of.

On his belt, his walkie-talkie came to life.

'Hello? Thomas?' the familiar voice asked. *'Is that you? Are you here?'*

The boy's expression dropped with panic.

. . .

The secret room was silent.

The footsteps Papy had heard had stopped.

Still with the walkie-talkie in his hand, he spoke into it.

"Thomas?" he said, nervously. "Please tell me that's you."

He unsteadily stepped forward, making his way over to the entrance, hoping the boy would run out to him, saying that the intruder had gone and all was well. But all that he could see was a mess of light and color as his eyes failed him.

Then something moved ahead.

He struggled to distinguish the shape that emerged in front of him. But as the shape got closer, it became larger. Much larger than Thomas was.

Papy stopped in his tracks.

"Who's there?" he said, shaky but loud, still with a finger pressed on the button of the walkie-talkie. "What do you want with me?"

No answer came from the advancing shape. Just the creak of the floorboards as it came closer.

Two floors above, in a tight stairwell that spiraled down into the bowels of the manor, Thomas was already running. The sound of his grandfather through the walkie-talkie was still crackling at his hip, distorted by static, broadcasting the trembling echo of a scared old man.

'*Who are you?*' Papy's said. '*Where is Thomas?*'

There was no answer to the old man's questions. Only the presence of the shape, now unmistakable in its outline: the red robe, the white beard, the glint of something metallic held tight in one hand.

The shape then chuckled. A slow, menacing sound.

As Papy took a step backward, his feet hit the first rung of the rope bridge. Not thinking about where he was going, only that it was away from this man, he rushed as fast as he could across it, which was not fast at all. As he moved, the whole bridge began to sway beneath him.

This absurd, swaying rope bridge, originally built for Thomas by his father, was suspended between two ends of the room like part of an obstacle course. Now it was the only escape open to Papy. He could not run left or right. Only back over this thing. His choices were either stay and face the shape or retreat and hope for survival.

The shape followed onto the rope bridge. Not

rushing like Papy was trying to do. There was no need. The old man blinked hard, trying to clear his vision, to fight his deterioration so he could see what was coming at him, but nothing worked.

"Take what you want," Papy pleaded. "Just leave us alone!"

The cake-serving knife rose in the man's hand.

"You are trying to stop me playing with him..." the voice from the shape said, sounding angry.

"No..." Papy whispered. "No, no..."

The old man turned to run faster, but as he did, he fell back into a wall. His escape route had come to an end, having run over the whole length of the rope bridge.

The blade in front of him was rising.

"Grandpa," the shape said, "I have my own game for you." His words were spoken with nothing but malice.

"Please..." Papy pleaded as he braced himself, shielding his face with both arms.

Before the blade could fall, the wall behind the old man gave way.

A panel slid open with a loud click, and Papy tumbled backward into the hole.

The man paused in surprise as Papy fell out of his view and the panel began to close once more.

Quickly, he lunged. Instead of striking any flesh, the knife's blade met with wood as the panel closed.

Papy was sprawled at the bottom of a small staircase, the sharp knife lodged deep in the panel they just came through.

Dazed and confused, the old man could not figure out what had happened before a pair of small hands grabbed him.

"Papy, it's me!" Thomas said, out of breath. His arms shook as he tried to help the old man to his feet. His panic making him clumsy. "It's Thomas, I've got you!"

As he pulled his relieved grandfather to his feet, they both hurried up the stairs as fast as they could.

Step after step they went until their route was blocked by another wooden panel.

Thomas opened it wide to reveal the inside of a wardrobe. As he pulled Papy in, his arm clipped the edge of the wardrobe's frame. It made a loud cracking sound as his armband monitor smacked onto the wood.

Thomas glanced down, stunned, at the now broken screen on his arm. Removing his view of the few camera feeds that remained.

He forced himself to focus. There were more important things at hand.

They got into the bedroom, and he quickly slammed the wardrobe door behind Papy, turning the lock into place.

"We gotta move," he urged quietly.

Together, they fled the room. Papy shuffling behind in exhaustion and panic, gripping onto Thomas' hand as he followed out of the room and into the hallway, toward the grand staircase.

But as they reached the top of the landing, Thomas stopped.

The door to the gym was wide open, as it always was.

Inside, it was dark. The benches and weight machines hidden in deep shadow.

He stared, thinking for a second.

The man in the Santa suit crashed through the wall panel. Breaking the wardrobe door off its hinges as he kicked his way out, the lock snapping off with ease.

As he stepped into the room, he turned to look back into the passage, to the stairs leading down to the hidden room full of toys.

But like Thomas, the man had to focus on the

matter at hand. The game.

Out of the room and down the hall he strode. His heavy boots pounding heavily as he went.

Getting to the top of the stairs, he too stopped outside the open door to the gym room, but unlike Thomas, he stopped not to think, but because he heard something coming from inside. Hardly even audible. More of a muffled whisper. A voice.

'I just need a moment to breathe...'

The man listened intently. He could hear the old man. A fragile, nervous, whispering voice. Coming from the gym.

Treading as quietly as he could the man walked through the dark room.

'He won't find us here,' the old man could be heard saying.

Scanning the dark gym with an intense gaze, he couldn't see anyone.

The voice spoke again, clearer.

'This house is enormous. Dozens of rooms like this one. I'm just slowing you down, you know.'

The man moved to the far end of the room. To the steam room, whose door was shut.

The whispering continued, getting clearer with each footstep. Coming from inside that room.

'Don't be silly, my dear boy,' Papy's voice could be heard saying. *'I have to stay here. I can't slow you*

down anymore. You have to escape. Now go. Call the police.'

Every step the man took was soundless as he reached for the handle.

'I've got nothing to lose anymore... I've had a long life.'

Yanking the door open, the man lunged inside, cake-serving knife swishing through the air at any target it could find. Not wanting to give the old man a chance to fight back.

But he was hitting nothing. The room was empty.

All there was, was the static sound, from on top of the bench inside. On top where a walkie-talkie sat.

Papy's voice drifted from its speaker, and now was closer. The man could hear a chuckle in his voice.

'Come on now, Thomas, stop crying. You're my little hero... Chin up.'

The man gritted his teeth, realizing that he was in a trap, but it was too late.

The door to the steam room slammed shut behind him.

He whirled to see, through the small circular window, Thomas staring right back at him, a look of victory on his face.

But the boy didn't say a word. Instead, and

without breaking eye contact, he slid a metal barbell from one of the many weight racks, through the handles of the steam room door, locking it firmly.

The man was also silent, glaring back at the boy.

Thomas then turned the small temperature dial on the wall. As he twisted it fully, warm steam started to erupt into the now-locked room.

The man looked in shock as the room began to fill. As the steam hissed in louder, getting hotter by the second, it started to fog the glass. The man could not hide his panic as he realized what was happening. He reached the door and rattled it violently, but it wouldn't budge. He stared once more through the small porthole window.

Thomas was still looking in, watching.

His young face, normally bright and boyish, now seemed much older. He looked at the man with a sadness, a hate and a disappointment. This Santa Claus, this ogre, this murderer of J.R. Here he was. Caught. Beaten.

Thomas shook his head as he turned and walked away, out of the gym and down the stairs to the lobby.

Hiding behind the suit of armor, Papy waited, still clutching and talking into his walkie-talkie.

"I'm staying," he spoke into it. "You run, Thomas. I'm done. Let him come to me. He—" his words stopped as he heard the pattering down the stairs.

"Hey," Thomas said, peering around the corner. "It worked, Papy ... You did great!"

"I can stop?" the old man asked, relieved.

Thomas quickly helped the old man to his feet.

"Come on," Thomas smiled. "We're getting out of here, okay? We can go find mom."

They walked together through the lobby and over to the front door.

But when Thomas reached for the handle, his stomach sank.

He had forgotten. The shutters had fallen into place. Over every door and room, he had accidentally activated them earlier. He glanced down at his armband monitor—his now broken armband monitor—and tried to hit the keys to deactivate them. But as he typed the code, he knew it would do nothing. And he was right. The connection had been broken.

He slapped the device with his palm. "Damn!" he grimaced.

"What is it?" Papy asked, startled by the boy's outburst, and still very much confused by everything.

"We can't leave the house."

"What do you mean, we *can't* leave?"

Thomas motioned to the door. "The shutters! They're locked."

Papy looked at the metal grate on the outside of the glass, then back at Thomas. He shook his head. "I have lived here for years, and there are big hidden rooms, now this? Am I dreaming, Thomas?"

The boy motioned to his armband. "This is the controller to open and close these, and it's broken."

"And?" Papy said. "So what? I really don't know what is happening..."

"Papy, please don't worry!" Thomas said. "It'd take too long to explain, but I'll think of something, okay."

The Porsche sped through the snow-covered narrow roads of the countryside, lined on each side by leafless trees that entwined overhead. The car drove faster than was legal or sensible.

Julie's hands were trembling on the wheel, as all the worst-case scenarios spiralled through her mind. Memories of what happened to her husband, terrible what-ifs of what could be happening now. She had spent so much money on making the house as safe as possible: alarms, security measures, CCTV, and given Thomas full control of it all. So that he could feel safe in his own home once more. She even hired a groundskeeper and a maid to always be on site, to oversee everything. But now, no one was answering her calls. And that made every terrible image play out in her mind—burglars, fire, flood, you name it— she now thought of it.

With the receiver held between her ear and her shoulder, she kept both hands on the wheel as she spoke to Roland. Her voice trembled with worry. "Roland, I can't do this anymore. It's been fifteen minutes and the line's still busy... I've tried everything. The private line, the gatehouse ... and nothing! No one is picking up."

As she spoke, the tears started, and she had no way of trying to stop them.

"I know *something's* happened," she sputtered, through quick breaths. "I *know* it. It's my fault. I shouldn't have left them alone... Just like last time... What if it's Papy? Maybe they took him to the hospital, he fell or had a heart attack, or didn't take his medication... that's why no one's answering!"

In the department store office, Roland kept his voice as calm as possible, trying his best to stop Julie unravelling on the line.

"Julie. Stop. Listen to me, okay?" he said as

calmly as he could manage. "If something had happened to your father, Thomas would've found a way to contact you. You *know* he would. It's probably just the phone line. Something simple. A fault. That's all... And it's really late." He could hear her about to retort, but he added quickly. "If it helps, I'll call the police, okay? Ask them to check the manor. Will that help?"

Julie did not answer right away, as she thought.

'No,' she eventually replied, trying her best to stop her breakdown getting more out of hand. *'I'll call them. They know me. You just please keep trying the house. Please.'*

"Of course," Roland nodded. "I won't stop, okay?"

After he hung up, he immediately dialed Julie's office phone.

As the line rang out its busy tone, he hung up and tried the main house line. A dead tone. Then the gatehouse, which just rang and rang.

Shaking his head, he looked up, into the dark office ahead of him, trying to think what to do. As he did, his eyes passed over the Minitel printer on the desk opposite. A length of perforated paper was hanging loose from its tray. A length that was not there earlier.

Having no recollection of printing anything, he

put the phone on the desk and walked over. Reaching for the paper he tore it free from the machine. The message stopped him cold.

Me and my grandfather are being attacked by Santa. He's an ogre now. Send help!
Please Send Help!
Thomas De Frémont

Roland stared at the words. He hoped that this was the boy playing a joke. Trying to get his mother back home. If that was the case, he would be in so much trouble, but at least he would be safe.

The lobby of the manor was now getting colder as the night wore on. Papy sat on a chair by the wall, wrapped in a heavy coat, trying to hold in his shivers. Thomas paced the marble floor nearby, his eyes darting across the room as he talked to himself under his breath.

"The attic windows aren't locked, but we can't jump... it's too far down." His brow furrowed deeper as he saw his limited options. "Can't break the windows, because of the shutters. Can't override the shutters from here as I stupidly altered the programming... Damnit..." he took a breath. "Only one option. I need to rewrite the system. Uncouple it from the locking system."

He stopped pacing, and turned to his grandfather.

"Papy. You need to hide, okay? Somewhere warm. You can't sit here freezing," he said. "This is gonna take some time."

Julie's fingers were white knuckled as the car still sped through the snowy country lanes.

"I need to speak to the chief of police, please..." she said into the phone. "What do you mean he's not available? Yes, I know what time it is, and I know it's Christmas, but this is an emergency!"

She exhaled loudly, as the voice on the other end of the call explained.

"Fine... My name is Julie de Frémont. I've been calling my house nonstop, and no one's answering. The staff aren't picking up either. I *know* something's happened. Please, please, can you go to my house right now?"

A pause as the voice asked a question.

"I won't be there for another 25 minutes, and I just know something terrible has happened. Please. *Please*. I'm begging you."

After giving her address to the police switchboard operator, Julie hung up the phone.

Before she had time to replace it onto the handset, the car's headlights flicked through the falling snow just in time to catch movement. A flash of leaping fur that crossed in front of her. A deer crossing through the snow.

Julie instinctively slammed the brakes as she let out a scream.

The tires squealed but lost all grip on the icy asphalt.

The Porsche skidded to the left as she swerved to avoid the animal, sliding across the road with a crunch of metal and the crack of breaking branches. It barreled through the trees before finally coming to a stop in a ditch at the side of the road.

After that... Silence.

Inside the car, with the airbag released, the dashboard light flickered in a fury. The car phone began to ring, but Julie couldn't answer.

She was unconscious.

Roland was standing at his desk on the phone, the printer paper with Thomas' message held tight in his hand.

The phone line was ringing.

"Come on, answer," he said impatiently.

The line then clicked as a robotic voice answered.

'The person you are trying to reach is not available. Please try again later.'

He quickly redialed, and the line rang for a while until it clicked off again.

'The person you are trying to reach is not available. Please try again later.'

Roland lowered the phone from his ear. Unsure of what he could do now. He didn't have his car, Julie was calling the police, no one at the house was answering... But now Julie was not answering.

He looked at the clock. 3:12am.

The Steam Room door groaned loudly, as with one last slam from inside, it cracked open. The weightlifting bar slipped from the handle to the floor, releasing the man, who came falling out. Steam billowed as he staggered to his feet, coughing and gasping for air.

The fake snow that colored his hair and beard had melted, and dripped down his face, making him look like a burned candle. His skin was mottled with burns, the steam having been turned up too high for safety. His face was contorted in pain. His eyes burned with a desperate confusion. Why would his new friend do this to him? His hurt then gave way to a much darker feeling of anger. A feeling of betrayal festered in him, quickly becoming hotter even than the steam that had blistered his skin.

He left the room and grabbed onto the staircase banister for support.

The snow continued to fall in a thick blizzard as, on his BMX, Pilou pedaled harder through the woods. Neither of his parents woke as he left the house. Tehy would have been furious if they knew. But somethings were more important.

His tires crunched on the path, as he hit the brakes, coming out of the treeline onto the De Frémont estate, slowing down near a parked Printemps delivery van.

With his attention on the manor ahead, he did not look at the gatehouse, or have any idea about what was inside it. Nor the dead body inside the van itself.

CHAPTER SEVEN

In the boiler room, the lowest level of the manor house, Thomas was crouched beside a metal panel stamped with the bold lettering *Secure-lock Inc.* A protective mask covered his face, as its visor reflecting sparks of light from the blowtorch in his hand.

He was just ten years old. Yet here he was, having already rewired the manor's security system and now using a power tool to access its core. What would worry most adults didn't bother him at all. To Thomas, this wasn't dangerous or difficult. It was simply logical. Almost easy.

In his hand, the blowtorch hissed against the casing, causing sparks to fly out around him. As he cut through the metal, he calmly guided the torch in a rectangular shape, until a cutaway fell out to the floor, exposing the security system circuitry beneath.

"As easy as one, two, three," he said as he reached for the wire stripper sitting on the floor next to him.

Within moments, wires had been removed, then reattached to different connectors. He didn't need a manual. He had the schematics in his head.

He had rewired this once before. He just had to put it all back to how it was, removing the wires he added, and handing back control to the main system.

The second the final connection was made and the wire twisted onto the connector, Thomas put down his tools and threw the master switch on the wall.

Somewhere deep in the house, mechanisms, servos, and cogs groaned to life.

One by one, on each door and window, the steel shutters began rolling back into their housing. The manor, having been sealed like a vault, was now open.

"It's done!" Thomas shouted, removing the mask.

He got up and ran from the lower basement to the lobby, calling out as he went. "It's fixed, Papy! We can go!"

But before he could reach the top stair, a hand shot from the side. The fingers wrapped around his ankle and yanked. The hand threw Thomas off his balance sending him careening to the floor, skidding across the marble as he landed hard.

As he thudded to the floor, the plastic knife from his boot was shaken loose from its scabbard and slid a few feet ahead of him.

In a daze, Thomas saw the knife fall and reached for it instinctively, but froze when he heard the noise of loud footsteps approaching.

Turning, he gasped as he saw the man in red. Santa Claus. The Ogre. Now over him, with a real blade raised. The still-bloodied cake-serving knife.

Thomas, caught in the impossible logic that was in front of him, looked from the man's real blade to the fake one on the floor in front of him, laying only a few feet away. For a second, he believed, desperately and irrationally, that the toy knife might be enough.

He scrambled for it.

But he was too slow for the man, who lunged forward.

A flash of steel, and the cake-serving knife sliced into the back of Thomas' thigh.

Blood immediately seeped through the fabric as the boy screamed.

He crumpled, clutching his leg, crying out from the pain.

The man in the Santa suit stepped closer,

looming, with a large smile on his face. Not a cruel or malicious one, but a genuinely happy one.

The man wanted to tell Thomas how much he was enjoying their game, but before he could, the front door swung open, and a blast of blizzard flew inward.

Pilou stood on the threshold.

His mouth fell open in shock as he took in the scene: Thomas bleeding on the floor crying out, the man in the costume, the gleaming knife in his hand.

"Run! Pilou," Thomas screamed. "Get out of here! *Run!*"

The man in the Santa suit immediately turned and charged toward the door. Toward the uninvited guest into the man's game. Toward Pilou.

His knife held out, swung at the boy.

But Pilou didn't hang around. He turned and bolted back into the snow, as the man gave chase.

His BMX was already in motion before Pilou's feet hit the pedals. Screaming in panic, he pushed himself forward with everything he had, flying over the frozen soil of the manor's driveway, wheels spinning on the gravel as he sped away, his body bent low over the handlebars.

Behind, the man thundered out of the front door, blade swinging furiously in the air.

Down into the gardens Pilou raced. The BMX pedals spinning around as fast as his strength allowed.

The snow did not relent as he turned the bike between the rows of neatly cut hedges.

The noise of the storm meant Pilou could not hear the man sprinting right behind him. Could not hear the gasping breaths and yells of anger.

He looked back once, barely able to see anything except the whiteness of the storm. But then he did it again.

That was one too many times, as his wheel slid and hit an icy patch of dirt.

The handlebars jerked sideways as the front tire slid out. Pilou went down as the bike bounced and skidded ahead on the path.

He did not wait to feel the pain that shot through his scraped leg as he scrambled back to his feet. Getting the BMX upright again. He did not have time to cry, as closing in behind him, the man in the Santa suit came nearer, one heavy step at a time.

"How dare you!" the man shouted, furious at the boy for interrupting.

Pilou got back on his bike and pedaled faster than he ever had in his life.

The man was getting closer and closer.

Off the garden path and onto the drive, the front gate shot past the boy. He didn't even register it as he sped by. He also didn't see the headlights until they were right there, a wall of blinding white to his right.

A car passed on the road outside, swerving and narrowly missing the bike.

But the man was not so lucky.

The vehicle clipped him, pushing him sideways, making him stumble backward.

Pilou didn't see any of it. He just kept riding out into the night, away from the nightmare that nearly caught up with him.

The passing car didn't stop either, leaving the man staring out, too far away now to catch the boy. The man's anger was now a feeling of helplessness. Would the boy now bring others to ruin his game? He couldn't wait any longer. The game had to be finished.

In the lobby, Thomas dragged himself inch by inch across the floor, blood streaking the tiles behind him. The wound on his thigh still bleeding thickly.

His hands soon gripped the base of the coat stand, and with a grunt of effort, he forced himself upright. The tears in his eyes almost blinding his view.

Papy's worried voice came from the shadows.

"Are you okay, Thomas? I can't see too well in here."

"I'm okay," Thomas said, breathing heavily, trying to mentally push away the pain stinging through his thigh. "It's nothing. I just fell."

The coat stand swayed as he gripped it harder to stand up straight.

"Don't move, okay?" he added, slowly losing control and blubbing through the words.

From inside the suit of armor, near the foot of the stairs, Papy's voice replied, muffled from within the metal.

"I wasn't planning on moving... But please, Thomas... are you okay?"

"I'll be back soon," the boy managed to say before he left the lobby and limped to the staircase, back down to the basement. Each step he took sent shocks up his body. The wound had soaked through his pants, but he pressed on, one hand on the rail, pulling himself down. He had to. He knew it was all up to him, and he could not let history repeat itself. It was time to go to war. Escape had not worked. There were no options left. But he was prepared.

When he finally got to his secret room, he turned on the computer array. The monitors lit up at once.

In the center of the desk, surrounded by bits of incomplete circuit boards, an old microphone waited.

He flipped the switches on the amplifiers, as the sound system came to life.

Upstairs, in the lobby, the man in the Santa suit had returned and was crouched at the coat stand. He had no idea who was now in the suit of armor nearby, and Papy was desperately trying to keep it that way, and remain quiet.

The man was too distracted picking up something that had fallen to the floor: a pair of military dog tags.

He turned them over in his fingers. Etched in the metal was the boy's name. THOMAS DE FRÉMONT. He stared at it and smiled. That was his friend's name, he thought. He would return them after their game.

From around him, from speakers hidden throughout the house, a voice rang out, breaking the silence. Thomas' voice.

'You don't know where I am, do you?'

The man stood and looked around, his eyes following the ceiling to where a speaker sat.

'You can't know. Because you don't know this house.'

Back in the secret room, Thomas held the microphone tightly.

His voice, when it came again, was different. Harder and focussed. He hated the fact he cried, and showed any weakness. He had prepared for this, and now he would fight the war with all he had.

"You're on my turf, Santa. And I swear you're going to regret ever stepping foot in here..." he took a moment to compose himself as he spoke the next words. He was intent on not showing any sadness to the ogre. "You killed my dog... You tried to kill my grandfather. You hurt me. All because I wanted to see you. That's all. You turned into an ogre, and I cannot allow that to happen."

He took a breath before continuing. "I'm angry. And I don't care if you're Santa Claus. I'm going to make you afraid of *me*... I'm going to make you regret that you ever came into my house. I'm going to punish you."

· · ·

A few minutes later, in the dull light of the secret room, Thomas was busily preparing as the man stalked the rooms above, one at a time.

After bandaging up his wound with an old t-shirt, Thomas grabbed an old, broken chair that lay nearby, and snapped the leg off from it. Tying it to his own wounded leg, he strapped it into a rough brace with some twine.

He tested the weight as he took a step forward. It was awkward, but it worked. Allowing him to walk without falling.

J.R.'s body lay on the dining room floor. Cold and with his tongue lolling out of his mouth.

From a panel in the wall, Thomas stepped out quietly, peering around to check that the man was not here.

The coast was clear.

Thomas tried to keep his tears inside as he gently lifted the body of his best friend down the stairs to the boiler room on the very bottom of the house. The only room with a dirt floor. A floor he could dig with his bare hands. A hole to bury J.R.

The memories were unbearable. The joy they

had shared had been stolen by Santa Claus. The beautiful joy that J.R. had extinguished by an ogre's cruelty.

When the hole was dug and filled in, it was then marked with the only thing Thomas had to hand. The plastic sword from his back, now buried into the earth in place of a cross or headstone.

Thomas wiped his face as he left the room.

It was time for war.

Back in the secret room, he dug through his shelves until he found what he needed: a handheld machine with a circular display and a blinking green dot. Taped to the front was the tracking beacon. He had hunted J.R. many times with this crude device. He had strapped the same beacon to his collar and let the dog run away, then used the tracking screen to find where he went.

Grabbing one of the Velcro-covered throwing stars, he peeled the back off it, and stuck it to the tracking beacon.

Then all he needed was his slingshot.

Downstairs, the man in the Santa suit had searched corridor after corridor. He had gone room to room, through each wing, and found nothing. He was tired and confused. The game should have been over by now, but he felt alone. Had his new friend left?

Despondent, he was about to turn back to the secret room, to check that again, when he turned into a corridor leading to the lobby, but instead he found a barricade. One that had not been there when he first walked down five minutes ago.

It was dark in the corridor, but he could see enough. It was a barricade made of pillows, cushions, and blankets stacked high on top of each other.

Before he could approach, a steel marble flew out from behind the barricade and struck him clean in the chest. He staggered back in shock and a shooting pain.

Another hit followed. This time on the cheek, making him yelp. He quickly raised his arms to shield his face, and turned his back to run.

Just then, as planned, Thomas launched the throwing star from his slingshot.

It flew fast and stuck to the red cloak as it hit the man, centered between the shoulder blades, making the man fall forward.

He growled as he turned and ran back toward the barricade, not wanting to retreat anymore. His arms were raised ready to attack.

But when he got there, there was no one on the other side.

Thomas had already vanished through a side door, crawled into the dumbwaiter in one of the rooms, and pulled on its chain, lifting him upward.

The mechanism of the small dumbwaiter groaned as it got to the second floor.

As Thomas stepped out, he checked the screen from the device strapped to his belt. The red cross in the centre of the screen was his position, and the green dot was the tracking beacon. They were far apart.

He smiled and hobbled down the hall, ready to set the next phase in motion. Traps he had spent years preparing for this exact moment. Since that night when everything changed. He could not be helpless again.

The ogre wouldn't see any of it coming.

Climbing the stairs, following the dumbwaiter's route up, the man started to hear it. The banging coming from above. With a smile he moved faster, past the first floor, up to the second where the noises got louder by the second.

. . .

Thomas slammed the door as hard as he could.

Opened, then slammed it again.

Over and over.

By the time the man reached for the door leading to the second-floor corridor, he was unluckily entering Thomas' planned warzone. The banging continued from the other side.

But it was too late. The moment his hand touched the knob, a jolt of electricity surged through him. Electrodes wired to the metal on the other side sent a harsh current through his body. He roared in pain, yanking his hand back as sparks snapped at his fingers. Staggering, he looked at the door in disbelief, clutching his seared hand.

Thomas wasn't finished.

The man's foot caught on the near-invisible tripwire stretched low across the hallway—a fishing line tied to a pulley rig. In an instant, a row of sharpened pencils, launched like crude spears, buried themselves into his ankles.

He cried out again, stumbling, only to trigger the next trap. Two toy crossbows, rigged on either side of the narrow passage, fired simultaneously. Six small darts thudded into his ribs and shoulder. He grimaced in pain and fury, shoving open the nearest door, desperate to escape this terrible onslaught.

Thomas had one more surprise waiting.

A hiss of liquid was his only warning. As the door swung open, a bucket perched overhead tipped forward. Hot cooking oil poured over his head and shoulders, soaking into his clothes and scalding his skin.

The man let out a scream that echoed around the house.

Even Papy, still hiding in the suit of armor, heard his cries.

In the shadows, Thomas laughed as he limped away, doing his best to ignore the throb in his leg. He moved fast, as fast as he could, heading back down hidden stairs, down to the boiler room.

The place where the next trap waited.

But even as he disappeared, the man in the Santa suit, burned, bleeding, and enraged, caught a glimpse of him going through a hidden panel in the wall ahead.

Pilou kept pedaling. It was not much further.

He did not go back home, there was no point, his parents would not believe him. They never did. So he headed to the only other place he could think of— the police station.

At the entrance to the boiler room, Thomas lay flat in cobwebs and dust, beneath the gappy slats of the floorboard. Floorboards that he had laid himself a year ago.

He had dug this hole years ago when Papy was more mobile and used to play hide and seek. It was not a place made for that game, but it was a place no one could find him, with the cracks between the floorboards that Thomas could see out of.

It was only a matter of time before the ogre stomped down the stairs, bleeding, scalded and dazed, still with the small darts stuck in his shoulder and ribs. The dripping fake snow that stained his brown beard and hair, turning it white, had now solidified, making his look of a dripping candle even more surreal and terrifying.

In his hand, the boy clutched another prepared weapon. One of his suction-cupped arrows. But not a usual one. One that had been coated in petroleum jelly and stored under the floorboards in an airtight box. That was not the only flammable item down here though, and the man dressed as Santa Claus could tell too.

The smell of gasoline was strong, and almost overpowering, but the man could not tell where it was coming from. As the fumes stung his eyes, he walked further into the room.

He did not notice the wetness in the dirt beneath his feet as he walked in, but he did see the empty canister lying ahead of him.

A clatter of wood caught his attention.

Thomas exploded up from beneath the floorboards, sending the loose slats flying around him.

A lighter in his hand quickly illuminated the jelly coated suction cup. Covering it in flames.

Moments later that arrow was flying.

The man had no time to react as it hit the floor in front of him and ignited instantly, boxing him in against the wall, facing a torrent of flame. They licked up his Santa Claus suit as the man screamed.

Thomas got up and ran back up the stairs. Ready to set the next trap. He did not worry about the fire spreading, he was more sensible than that. This boiler room was concrete lined and when the door was shut, trapped the fire inside.

The man, desperately gasping, tried to batter the flames with his hands.

. . .

"Please, listen to me!" Pilou shouted at the police officer sitting at the reception desk. "I saw him! He had a knife!"

"Santa Claus tried to stab your friend?"

"Yes, Thomas de Frémont!" Pilou could not believe he just said that, but he had no other explanation.

The policeman's expression dropped. "de Frémont?" he said, remembering when years ago he had to go to the manor in the middle of the night.

Immediately he picked up the phone and dialed an internal number.

"Sergeant, that crank call we got earlier? Saying she was Julie de Frémont... I don't think it was a joke... Okay, I'll send someone to check it out."

The man in the Sant Claus suit staggered to top of the stairs. Coughing as his charred suit smoked from the burning trap he had just escaped from. His hair was singed. His will was almost gone. His body was racked in pain, from darts, pencil tips, burning oil, and flames. Not to mention his hands aching from the recent electrocution.

As he stood in the lobby, his body wavering to

stay upright, he hesitated, with a charred palm resting on the jamb.

He looked ahead, worried and taken aback, as a small red train traveled up the corridor toward him. A small, wooden, wind-up toy now chugging nearer.

But he did not get worried by it, as he probably should do. When he saw the train, his posture changed. Something inside softened. He could not hold back a smile. A smile of childhood wonder.

The train continued its path. Its little wheels engaged with a soft whir, clacking over the floorboards, as somewhere from inside, a small lullaby played. A delicate and mechanical tune, like one from a music box, lilting faintly into the air.

The injured man could not help but let out a giggle.

In these shadows, he could not see the plastic grenade taped to the back of this toy. A grenade that had been filled with gunpowder from old fireworks, along with metal balls and a long trailing cloth strip. A strip that was a fuse that led to a lighter, wired to the front of the locomotive. One that when the lighter touched something, would spark, and ignite, giving only seconds before the grenade would explode.

The man saw none of that. He just saw the toy.

He crouched down with a look of wonderment as the train got to him.

He reached out to pick it up, just before the lighter had any chance to touch his boot, to spark the fuse.

The lullaby continued to play out from within this weapon's wooden body, as he stood up and studied the train, turning it over in his hands. Oblivious to the weapon it was.

He grabbed the large key on the train's side and began to wind it up.

He then placed the train carefully back onto the floor, facing away from him.

The wheels on the train turned, carrying it back the way it had come. The lighter on the front still sticking out, waiting to touch something, waiting to ignite the fuse.

The lullaby continued as the wheels clacked over the floorboards.

It traveled along the tiles, by the base of the Christmas tree where Thomas was now hidden. His breath caught as the weaponized toy trundled on past him, headed straight for the other side of the room, straight for the suit of armor. Straight for where Papy was hidden.

Panic surged in the boy. If the lighter struck the

base of the armor, it would light the fuse, the grenade would explode, and Papy...

No.

Thomas burst out from his hiding place with the sole thought of saving his grandfather. His boots skidded across the wood as he hobbled toward the train.

By the other side of the room, the man saw him and immediately gave chase. Despite his injuries, he let out a laugh. The game was on once more.

The boy sprinted, as best he could with his splintered leg, but the man was too fast, and the lobby was too small.

A powerful arm slammed into Thomas' side and took him down as the man in the Santa suit smashed into him.

His shoulder hit the floor first, then his chest. The wind pushed out from his lungs.

"No!" he cried out, still staring at the train heading to Papy.

"I caught you," the man shouted, oblivious to Papy or the train.

Ahead of them, the train struck the base of the armor with a hollow clink.

Thomas gasped.

The man laughed, thinking he had won finally.

The lighter on the train immediately flared to life.

A single flame licked the fuse. It caught instantly. That part of the mechanism worked perfectly.

The cloth burned quick.

Thomas flinched, bracing for the blast. Suddenly distraught that the worst was about to happen.

"Papy," he cried.

But all that came next was a soft cough of smoke. A pale, unimpressive cloud that drifted up into the air. No fire. No shrapnel. Just a spurt.

He lay for a second, heart pounding, then let out a shaky breath of relief that his trap had failed. The bomb hadn't worked.

The man above him, still smiling, shifted his weight and turned his attention back to the train. His walked over, and with his burned fingers, grabbed the toy, lifting it by its roof.

A final puff of smoke dribbled out.

Then his expression changed.

He turned the train over... and there, fixed with a strip of tape, was the plastic grenade. His eyes widened in a jolt of understanding. He had not seen it before as he was too enchanted with the toy itself, but now he could not ignore the bright silver plastic grenade shimmering in the half-light.

He looked at it confused. Then to Thomas, in

hope that the boy could explain what was happening.

But Thomas was already gone.

One of the Porsche's rear tires spun helplessly in the mud, flinging sludge behind it as Julie gripped the wheel, blood dripping from her cheek. The impact had thrown her into the steering wheel, cutting and dazing her. Her whole face was wrought with pain and frustration, as the dashboard blinked weakly at her.

She pressed on the accelerator again, hoping for the vehicle to move. But there was nothing that could be done. The wheels spun, but were stuck.

Behind her, a small delivery van screeched to a halt on the roadside. Catching it in the rearview mirror, she could not stop her smile as she recognized the word printed on the side: *Printemps*.

Roland leapt out of the van before the engine had finished rattling, sprinting across the icy road to the Porsche, whose tail was jutting out over the ditch. There was no way he could have missed her, as the taillights flickered, like a lighthouse in the storm.

He reached the side of the car, panting.

"Julie! Are you okay?" he asked in worry as he saw her bloodied face.

"Yes... I'm fine," she nodded. Despite her condition, she was only concerned with one thing. "Did you get through to them?" she asked.

He didn't answer. He was too busy looking at the car's wheels deep in the icy mud, already assessing the angle of the ditch she was in.

"Stay there," he said, walking around the front of the Porsche. "I'll get you out, okay?"

"*Roland,*" she shouted. "Please, did you call them?" Her voice was haunted with worry.

But he still didn't answer, not yet.

"Reverse now," he said, as he braced himself and put his hands on the front of the car, pushing.

A police cruiser crept through the open gates of the manor, its lights flashing in red and blue. It came to a halt beside the abandoned Printemps delivery van parked near the gatehouse.

From the vehicle, a single officer stepped out, his silhouette lit by the flashing. He looked around at the snow-covered grounds, then at the van.

Slowly, he approached it.

Inside the lobby, the man in the Santa outfit stood at the ground-floor window, pulling the curtain back just enough to watch as the flashing lights came through the gates.

His face was expressionless, eyes fixed on the officer.

He let the curtain fall, as he closed his eyes. Another person trying to stop the game.

Above, through a different window on the first floor, Thomas held his breath behind a pair of binoculars. From his perch, he could make out the shadow of the officer walking over to the van.

A spark of hope flickered in him, as he worried about Papy, stuck in the armor, probably terrified about all of this.

In the armor, the old man was not terrified. He was not awake. He had been in and out of consciousness within the metal cocoon for the past thirty minutes, and not from exhaustion.

Thomas half-ran, half-limped, as the makeshift chair-leg splint strapped to his wounded leg slowed him down. He did not think about what he was doing. He was just overjoyed the police had arrived. He had checked the locator, and the green dot was far away from the lobby now.

"They're here, Papy!" he said in an enthusiastic whisper as he got to the staircase. "We're saved! The police are here! I told you they'd come!"

He reached the lobby and rushed over to the suit of armor.

Thomas fumbled with the catches on the suit's side, trying to get his grandfather out of there.

But something was wrong.

From inside the suit, Papy made a strangled, gurgling sound. His breath was stilted and weak.

Thomas could see his grandfather's slowly blinking eyes through the metal slats of the mask.

"Papy? What's going on? Talk to me!"

Between gasps, a word finally formed.

"...insulin..."

Out on the driveway, the officer moved cautiously to the house, his sidearm raised. He was pale, having seen the body in the van, and the two through the window of the gatehouse.

This was not a false alarm as the station had presumed. He had made sure to call it in, but backup was not close, and he was here alone.

The manor was ahead, as he cautiously crept

through the snow. Each step crunched beneath him, louder than he would have liked. Around him the blizzard had calmed, and everything was eerily silent.

A twig snapped to his left, catching his attention.

He turned, swinging his gun around in a panic.

But he could see nothing there except the lightly falling snow and the darkness of the grounds.

He stared into the tree line, cautiously.

He did not see the sneering man in the Santa suit, burned, battered and bruised, creeping up from behind him.

CHAPTER EIGHT

Thomas limped along the first-floor hallway to his grandfather's bedroom. He went inside and hobbled to the bathroom, straight to the medicine cabinet. With his hands trembling, he opened it. Boxes spilled out as he desperately looked for the insulin.

He did not notice the tiny screen at his hip showing the green dot moving. It was no longer far away; it moved in, closer and closer to the red cross in the middle of the screen. The red cross that marked where he was.

He fought to calm down, to think clearly, to stop shaking and to find what he was here to find.

Finally, at the back of the cabinet, there it was: the box of insulin.

He grabbed it and opened the lid, but it was empty.

Before he could curse his bad luck, a low, whirring hum sounded from behind. Coming from the doorway.

Turning, he yelped as a small radio-controlled tank bumped against his foot. On its back, stuck on with tape, was the same tracking beacon attached to the Velcro-covered throwing star.

It was attached to this plastic toy.

He stood still.

"No," he whispered, knowing exactly what it meant.

He looked up and fearfully waited for the man to appear in the doorway.

Seconds ticked by...

...Then a full minute.

The house sat in silence as Thomas stood in worry. But the doorway ahead of him remained empty.

He didn't move. *Couldn't* move. Though every instinct screamed to run, to hide, to do something. He was just too scared. He could only stand, staring at the doorframe, waiting.

He must have stood there for at least five minutes. Listening. Breathing. Dreading.

And yet... no one came.

Finally, he forced himself forward, away from

the cabinet. He crept to the door and leaned out just enough to peer into the hallway.

There was no one to his left.

Before Thomas could breathe a sigh of relief, a hand reached out from and clamped over his mouth. Another hand pressed the cake-serving knife to his throat.

Thomas tried to fight back but the man in the Santa suit, the ogre, was just too strong.

"No," the boy tried to scream, but it came out as just a muffled whimper.

The man looked at the boy. The battles had taken their toll. He wheezed as he leaned closer to the boy in his grasp.

His voice was strained.

"I win," he said with a growing smile. "You *lose*..." he leaned in so close that Thomas could smell the man's rotten breath. "Now it's my turn to hide... and yours to find me... okay?"

Slowly, he lowered the blade and let Thomas go.

The boy looked terrified and confused as the man threw him face first against the wall.

"Count to twenty," he ordered. "And no cheating."

The man stormed off with a laugh, his heavy steps echoing down the hallway as he went.

Thomas whispered to himself, unsure of what

else he could do, "One... two... three..." he counted, with a tearful voice.

When he got to twenty, he had no idea what to do, why Santa Claus was doing this. But he still had to save Papy.

He only had one way to go now.

Only one place left to find the medication.

He made his way back downstairs as quietly as he could, wincing as his thigh ached.

Through the lobby, he passed the suit or armor.

"You're gonna be fine, Papy," he sobbed softly as he headed straight for the door. "I'll find your insulin!"

He hobbled down the steps, and onto the drive. Snow flitting at his face. His leg stung with every movement, the wooden splint barely doing much anymore as the strapping had started to loosen.

Everything seemed to be slowing him down. Everything on him felt heavy.

He tore the band from his head, discarded the belt around his waist, the tracking box... Anything weighing him down was dropped as he made his way across the drive to the flashing lights of the police car by the gatehouse. Lights that seemed so far away, much further than they actually were.

But he was not here for the police. His attention

was locked on the only thing that mattered: getting to the gatehouse.

As he got closer, he could not see anyone. But he didn't have time to worry about that. He had his mission.

Inside the gatehouse, Thomas flung open the door and leaned inside.

"Hello?" he said. "Is anyone here? Charles? Linda?"

He didn't notice the bodies slumped in the living room. He didn't see the blood that washed over the carpet.

When no answer came. He hobbled across to the delivery room. The small room where the parcels were sorted before being brought over to the manor.

He quickly clawed through several boxes searching for the one. He did not stop at the toy boxes that were there.

It was not long before his hands found it.

Tearing open the lid, there they were. Ampoules of insulin.

He cried once more, this time with joy.

. . .

The police car door was thrown open, and seeing the keys still in the ignition, Thomas climbed in. The lights above still spinning, illuminating the grounds around it in red and blue, but there was no officer in sight.

He could not walk the distance back to the house, it was too much with the pain in his leg getting worse. He had to do something else.

Just like he had done in the Ford Taunus, he turned the key.

Moving the seat as far forward as it would go, he reached his good leg down and jammed on the gas pedal.

The engine sprang to life as the car jerked forward, swerving down the snowy path to the manor. It was a car that was much more powerful than the Ford, more so than Thomas was used to.

He grabbed the radio handset, and pressed on the talk button.

"Hello? Police! Do you copy? Please... Someone... I need help!"

A second passed.

Then: "Hello? Please repeat and identify yourself. Over."

"I'm Thomas de Frémont. A man has attacked us... Please send an ambulance to—"

He stopped mid-sentence, as a hand reached out from the back seat.

Thomas saw the glimpse in the rearview.

There in his hiding place in the back seat, was the man in the Santa suit.

The ogre.

The murderer.

"Cheater," the man hissed. "*You are a cheater.*"

Thomas dropped the radio and let go of the wheel, as the man's hand grabbed his collar.

On the snowy drive, the wheel banked hard to the right as the wheels slipped. The whole vehicle spun around, and the man was flung sideways into the door, his hand losing grip on the boy.

The car veered out of control, skidding until it slammed into a tree with a heavy crunch.

On impact, without a seatbelt on, Thomas was hurled forward, his forehead smacking hard against the windshield before he crumpled back into the seat.

The Porsche had been pushed out of the ditch, and was now making its way along the road. In the passenger seat, Julie wept openly, her hands clenched in her lap holding the printout that Roland had received in his office.

He drove in silence.

There was nothing either of them could say.

The lights still rotated on top of the wrecked police car, their glow spinning slower as the power in the car's battery now dissipated from the crash.

Smoke seeped out from the vehicle's crumpled hood.

In the driver's seat, Thomas was coming to.

Blood trickled down his face from his hairline.

Behind him, he heard a moaning. A pained exhalation.

The man in the Santa suit was also waking. Having fallen into the footwell, he was now wedged between the front and back seats. He clawed at the handle above the door, desperately reaching for it to pull himself up.

Noticing, Thomas knew that he had to act fast. He remembered the only thing he did not drop to the floor as he ran, the plastic handcuffs that were stuffed in his pocket. He reached for the cuffs and lunged over the seat. Looping one end of the cuffs through the handle, Thomas then fastened the other around the man's grasping wrist.

The man screamed in a rage, but Thomas didn't wait around. He grabbed the insulin that rested on the passenger seat and pushed open the door. Falling out into the snow, he clutched the medication tightly, and got to his feet.

He had closed half the distance to the manor when he heard the police car door slam behind him, as the man tore his way out from his restraints.

His leg throbbed with every step, his splint slipping further the more he walked on it. But Thomas didn't stop. He would never forgive himself if he did. Papy was waiting for him. Relying on him.

He also didn't see what was on the ground in front of him until it was too late. His foot caught on something large across the path, and he went sprawling over it. Pain shot through his wound as he collapsed. The box of insulin falling a few feet away.

His screams of pain were eclipsed by the bellowing laughter coming from behind him.

The thing he'd tripped over wasn't a tree or a rock. It was a body. The body of the policeman. The *dead* body of the policeman. With his head turned one hundred and eighty degrees, he faced the sky as his body was in the opposite direction.

The man in the Santa suit was still laughing as he walked closer. His steps as unsteady and pained as Thomas'.

But the boy was not looking at the body, nor the man. His eyes had locked onto something else, just beyond the body. A police issue revolver that must have fallen from the officer's belt.

Thomas quickly lunged, grasping it tightly as he rolled onto his back and aimed the gun at the man in the Santa suit.

With his arms outstretched, he could not stop the weapon from trembling in his grip. He was terrified and furious all at once, but instead of firing, his lips trembled.

"Why...?" he whimpered as he burst into floods of tears. "Santa Claus is supposed to be kind."

The man stood and his laugher disappeared. Something quickly changed in his expression. He looked worried.

"Oh no," the man said as he stepped forward, reaching out to the boy, seeing that he was genuinely upset. "I didn't mean—"

The shot rang out like a thunderclap throughout the grounds. Louder than the storm that fell upon it.

The man staggered, shocked and confused as he

collapsed down onto the snowy dirt. A dark bloom of red spreading across his coat.

Thomas crawled to his feet, then turned and moved as fast as he could to the house, picking up the box of insulin along the way. The revolver still in his grasp.

"Papy...? Are you okay?" Thomas asked as he approached the suit of armor.

But no response came from inside.

Not even the rattling breath from earlier.

Panic rising, he dropped the gun to the floor and reached for the clasps on the side. But like before, he could not open them. The metal was too old and rigid for his small hands to have the strength to open.

He then heaved, seeing no other choice available to him, pulling with all his weight, until the armor leaned forward and fell. Crashing to the floor with a deafening clatter. But inside, Papy still didn't stir.

Sobbing once again, Thomas dropped to his knees and rolled the heavy frame over with all his might.

Reaching for the helmet, Thomas' small hands held the clasps. It took everything he had to pry just one open. But as it clanked, the helmet came off.

Papy's eyes were closed. He was still. Breathing so shallowly.

"No," Thomas whispered. "No, no, no... Papy, please. I'm here!"

Thomas then reached for the clasps on the body of the armor. Thankfully, the fall had made them weaker, and they soon opened.

When the chest plate was finally removed, Thomas shook his grandfather gently, but there was no response. The old man looked so fragile in his pajamas, his face pale and still.

Heart pounding, Thomas reached for the insulin. With trembling hands, he pulled out an ampule and a syringe. He tore open the packaging, removed the needle's sheath, and slid the point inside the bottle to draw out the liquid.

He had done this countless times before. But now, everything felt unfamiliar, like it was his first time. His fingers fumbled as he pulled up his grandfather's pajama top and pushed the needle into his abdomen.

He pushed the plunger down.

All that he could do now was wait.

Outside the snow fell, and something bloodied now moved.

. . .

"Breathe," Thomas begged. "Please breathe."

The wait seemed like an age.

He pounded his tiny fist onto his grandfather's chest, as the sobs came again.

"Breathe! Please! Don't die... I can't lose you too..."

Today was not that day, though, as Papy lightly coughed as he started to wake up. He was weak and breathing shallowly, but getting stronger.

Thomas broke down. He hugged his grandfather, clutching him like a lifeline. Relief hit so hard, that he could barely focus.

"It's okay... breathe..." he cried. "Papy... you're okay... I got your insulin for you."

But as hope crept in, something else did.

Something in the doorway that caught the boy and old man's attention.

There, bent over, gripping his bleeding stomach, was the man in the Santa suit. The ogre. The murderer.

He stood at the threshold of the house. He was caked in snow and blood. His skin was blistered and bruised. His suit was torn and frayed. His boots dragged behind him, and his eyes were sunken as he stared at Thomas in hopeless despair. The fake snow that caked and coloured his beard and hair was smeared and cracking off him in chunks.

He lifted one hand to the boy.

Not to strike. Not to attack. But a plea for help.

"No!" Thomas cried, getting to his feet. Standing between his grandfather and the man. "Stay away!"

The old man, still weak, turned his head. Though through blurred vision, he saw one figure in front of him and another in the doorway. Slowly, painfully, he began to crawl to the nearer one, presuming it must be his grandson. As he did his fingers passed over the fallen revolver.

"Please... go away!" Thomas screamed at the man now lumbering toward him, reaching out for mercy, yet looking like a demon grasping for Thomas' soul.

Papy's hand closed on the grip. But when he raised the gun, his vision continued to betray him. Everything was blurred. All he could see were two figures, both now moving, but had no idea who was who. Which was Thomas? Which was the intruder?

He hesitated, as he started to worriedly moan.

Then he saw it. A flash of red.

He didn't think. He just shouted, "Thomas, get on the floor now!"

The gun then went off.

. . .

Through the gates, the Porsche sped into the estate, headlights shining across the delivery van, as it picked up speed in the direction of the manor.

As it did, it soon passed the police car, crashed against the tree.

Roland and Julie looked out, stunned, the dread plainly written across their faces.

In the glow of the Christmas tree in the lobby, Thomas stood, staring down at the dead body of Santa Claus.

The red coat.

The black boots.

The expanding pooling blood darkening the floorboards.

He did not feel victorious about this as his mind replayed the words he'd heard.

'*He doesn't exist,*' Pilou had scoffed.

'*They never found his skeleton, did they?*' Thomas had whispered.

'*That's because Santa isn't dead. Obviously...*' Papy had explained.

And then his own voice, full of conviction, rang in his memory:

'*I'll prove he's real.*'

'*Get down, Thomas!*'

'*Nooo.*'

The gunshot still echoed in his head, as he looked at the proof of everything in front of him.

'*You know, you shouldn't try to see Santa Claus. If you do, he gets angry. And then... he turns into an ogre.*'

Julie and Roland rushed in, hearts pounding, eyes darting, until they saw it all at once.

Papy, there collapsed on the floor, gun still in his hand.

Thomas, stood over a dead Santa.

Roland dropped to his knees beside the old man, as Julie went to her son and pulled him into her arms.

She held him tightly, cradling his face, kissing his hair, whispering things he could barely hear.

"Thomas... my little boy... it's over now. It's over..."

He didn't answer right away. His gaze was still fixed ahead, at the dead man in red.

Then, slowly, he turned to his mother. His voice a whisper.

"It's my fault... I just wanted to see him... And you told me he would... He turned into an ogre. All because of me. And now J.R. is... He..."

Julie wrapped him tighter in her embrace.

Outside, sirens wailed out in the distance, as police cruisers and ambulances finally approached.

Five minutes later, four officers had come into the house, weapons drawn, followed by Pilou.

The lobby was soon filled with people.

But Thomas didn't move, didn't stop staring at Santa Claus.

He kept waiting to see if the body would twitch, if a hand would claw free. If the man would come back again. But there was nothing.

The boy, who only hours ago had been a soldier, a commando, a warrior in a game of pretend, now looked impossibly small in the reflected lights that came through the door.

His mother still held her son, not wanting to let go, as Papy—who had been helped to his feet by Roland—came over.

Then finally, Thomas said what he felt. "Mom... I killed Christmas..."

He then collapsed into her arms. All the strength, all the resolve, everything he had held together through the night dissolved in that one moment.

Her hands cradled the back of his head, rocking him gently as if he were a baby again.

As the police took the body away, Thomas was beside his mother in the dining room, a blanket around his shoulders, his leg bandaged up by a paramedic.

He stared out into nothing, a thousand thoughts colliding behind his eyes. Julie stroked his hair, worried. She had been told about what had happened. About Charles and Linda. About the Printemps delivery driver. About the policeman. About J.R.

She could not fathom how this happened. And how her son and father had come through it.

Outside, the sun broke faintly through the clouds, as morning started to arrive.

Wind blew over the manor, up over the slate tiles. The snow up there lay untouched except for one thing: a steel grappling hook, still anchored on the roof's edge. The last trace of the myth that had come, uninvited, and tried to make itself real.

It was now Christmas morning, and it would be lunchtime before the emergency services would finally leave the manor and the gatehouse. But when they did, Thomas asked for a moment to himself.

Julie reluctantly agreed as her son hobbled off on his new crutches, down the stairs into the basement.

Papy stood by and whispered. "Did you know he has a secret room of toys and machines down there?"

"Of course I do," Julie said with a weak smile. "Who do you think goes in there and cleans it when he's at school?"

Thomas sat in front of his monitors, the few cameras not destroyed still displayed on some of the screens. Every one of Thomas' traps had been triggered. Every plan he conceived to protect the house put into action. And despite all that... J.R., Linda, Charles, and more... all gone. He may have saved himself and Papy, but he did not save everyone.

All that preparation, yet people still died.

He looked at his machines. He knew now that he was not invincible. That war was not a game. And as he saw the man in the Santa suit looking at him helplessly, he now knew that nothing was totally evil. He saw the humanity in that man. The pain in his eyes. The plea for mercy. But even so, Thomas could not understand it.

He reached up and turned the system off, with no intention to ever turn it back on again.

He'd built traps, devised attacks, set up surveillance… but in the end, Thomas understood: he was only a child, and this had always been a man's war.